'Tis The Season

A HOLIDAY ANTHOLOGY: 2022 SEASON

TEXAS SISTERS PRESS

Contents

'Tis The Season, A Holiday Anthology; 2022 Season

I t's that time of year again - the annual Texas Sisters Press Holiday Anthology! Each year we have some spectacular authors enter their holiday-themed short stories for you to enjoy, and this year is no exception. So, grab you cup of hot cocoa, curl up on the couch, and enjoy these heart-warming holiday stories:

The Christmas Contest by Barbara Arent
A Family Christmas by Diann Floyd Boehm
Lost And Found by Terry Korth Fischer
Charlie The Menace by DC Gomez
A Long Winter's Nap by Sherry Hall
A Rose By Another Name by Kathryn Haueisen
The Year Christmas Came Early by LM Mann
A Chaos Christmas by Mandy McCool
The Christmas That Almost Wasn't by C.J. Peterson
Deck The Halls by Veronica Smith
Alone At Christmas by Teresa Trent

THE CHRISTMAS CONTEST

BY:

BARBARA ARENT

Author Barbara Arent

Barbara Arent lives in the Piney Woods of East Texas surrounded a large loving family. A graduate of the Children's Institute of Literature, she has been writing stories for years and been published in her Sunday school paper.

You can find her online at:

https://www.amazon.com/Barbara-Arent/e/B00ARI6T9Q

The Christmas Contest

⌒⌒⌒

Tracy Leaman closed her eyes and fought the urge to throat-punch the next person who walked through the door and said Merry Christmas. The doorbell jingled, she looked up and Mika Alle – who owned the hardware store next door - walked in. A smile stretched across her face. If anyone in the small town of Buzbee could counter a throat-punch, he could.

Mika looked around. "Merry. . ." He stopped when he looked straight at her. "What are you smiling about?"

"My martial arts training, I really need someone to train with. Want to volunteer?"

A suspicious look planted itself on his face. "Uh, no."

"Why not?"

"Because, you're what – five-six, a hundred and ten pounds soaking wet." He waved his hand in front of his six-two, two hundred and twenty pound body. "I'm about twice your size."

She frowned. "Think I'm not tough enough?"

"Oh, you're tough enough." Mika grinned. "You probably know some secret move to put me on my knees. Then you'd throat-punch me. I'd be on the floor gagging. Game over.

Everyone in Buzbee would know exactly what happened." He shrugged. "Embarrassing to say the least."

"You seriously think that?"

"More like know it." He leaned against the counter. "Now out with it. You had a real smile on your face, and I want to know why."

Tracy shook her head. "Why are you here?"

"I'm heading to Jacob's Tree Lot tonight to get a tree for my shop. Want to go?"

"I wasn't planning on putting up a tree.

He leaned his elbows on the counter –his face close enough to see the green flecks in his eyes. She eased back.

"The Christmas decoration contest is important to me. To win, all the shops on this block have to decorate. And since we're the only two shops on this block, you have to participate." He wondered over to the front window. "If we got a small tree, we could move some of this stuff around and set it in the window. I already have a space for mine."

"You know my thoughts about all the Christmas glitz."

He turned and held his hands about three feet apart. "Just a small one. A few lights. It doesn't have to be anything fancy."

"Don't you have a store to run?"

"Steve's working this afternoon so I can go home and get stuff to decorate with." He put a hang-dog look on his face. "But if you're not willing to decorate, it won't do me much good."

Tracy snorted. "Three brothers, remember? That look will get you nowhere."

He sat down on the smaller stool behind the counter which put them face to face. "I haven't had lunch yet. You?"

She shook her head. "Too, busy."

He pulled out his cell phone and punched in a number. "Fay, it's Mika. Tracy and I missed lunch. Can we still get our usual?"

She shook her head again.

"I'll be there is three minutes."

Tracy poked him. "I don't want lunch, especially if you're buying."

He placed his hand over his heart. "That hurt deep."

"Like anything I say would hurt your feelings. Don't you have stuff to go get?"

He stood and headed for the door. "Yep, lunch."

He was out the door before she could say more. She sighed. Fay was the biggest gossip in Buzbee. Shoot, in the three surrounding counties. Before the afternoon turned into evening, she'd tell everyone Mika and Tracy had a lunch date. She felt like locking the door and sneaking out the back.

The bell over the door jingled, and her mother walked in. Tracy's heart sank. Mika would be back with lunch in five minutes. When her mom saw Mika in the store, she would think they were dating, have them married and presenting her with grandchildren in a week.

"Hey, Mom, what are you doing here today?"

"Well, daughter of mine, I came to ask you to spend the weekend with me in Amarillo. Maybe take in a local play." She walked behind the counter and ruffled Tracy's hair. "A spa day, shopping, a little girl time."

"Mom, you know I can't go right now. This is the busiest time of the year for me."

The doorbell jingled and Mika came in. Her mother smiled and arched an eyebrow at her. Tracy contemplated bolting out the back door.

Mika set a sack and the drink carrier on the counter. He handed her a cup. "I got you tea." He trotted out his thousand watt smile for her mother. "Mrs. Leaman, nice to see you. What brings you to town?"

Tracy blinked, thankful he never directed that smile at her. Her mother almost simpered.

"I've come to steal my daughter away for the weekend but she claims she is too busy right now."

Mika nodded. "That is correct, Ma'am" He pointed at the

7

sack. "We've been so busy neither of us had lunch." He set out her food. "There should be enough for both of you ladies." He'd picked up his. "I left Steve alone at the counter. I better get back."

Tracy scowled at his retreating back.

"Such a nice young man."

"I suppose he is, Mom, but I don't know him that well."

"He works right next door." Her mother frowned. "Please tell me you're not ignoring a handsome man that's practically been dropped in your lap."

Tracy started laughing. "Mom, you want lunch?"

The bell jingled, and Mika walked in. Tracy frowned. There was no reason for any man in a pair of ragged jeans and an old stained T-shirt to look as good as he did.

"Is the coast clear?"

"I gather you're referring to my mother?"

"Nice lady, but she's more intimidating than you are."

Tracy laughed. "You almost had her drooling with that smile, and she intimidated you?"

"She is your mom, and any mother that raised a smart, tough woman like you has to be intimidating."

She shook her head. "It's closing time. What are you doing here?"

"Christmas trees, remember?"

"We didn't finish discussing Christmas trees because you bugged out. I never said yes."

"True, but you didn't say no, either."

Tracy shook her head. "It's been a long day. I'm going home, fix a cup of hot chocolate, wrap up in a blanket and go sit outside to look at the stars."

"Asking nicely didn't do it. Looking pitiful didn't do it." Mika gave out a deep sigh. "The contest is important." He opened the door and waved for someone to come in. "So, I brought back up."

"Hello, dear."

Tracy schooled her face. If she'd been closer to Mika, she would have used that secret move to put him on his knees and throat-punched him. No one in town would refuse Mika's mom anything. "Mrs. Allen."

"Mika promised me pizza if I'd come tonight." She smiled at Tracy. "Although, I'm not sure why. It's not like you two need a chaperone."

"No, Ma'am, unless you are here to keep me from doing your son bodily harm." Tracy moved beside Mika, pinched the back of his arm, and gave him her sweetest smile. At least she hoped it looked sweet.

Mrs. Allen frowned at Mika. "Why would Tracy hurt you?"

"Mom, she just pinched me." He rubbed his arm. "I'll probably have a bruise for a week."

"Mrs. Allen, I don't really do Christmas, and Mika knows that. But he has his heart set on winning the town Christmas decoration contest. For him to win, I have to decorate also."

"Ah, I gather you didn't agree to either decorating or going to the tree lot."

"No, ma'am."

"In my defense, Mom, Tracy didn't say no either"

Tracy shoved him with her shoulder. "That's only because my mom showed up, and he ran like his shirt tail was on fire."

"Ida was in town? I hate that I missed her." Mrs. Allen glanced between them and turned toward the door. "Evidently, we have a lot to discuss."

Tracy frowned at Mika. "Who has a lot to discuss?"

He shrugged. "Probably you two. Mom goes all out at Christmas. She could have this place decorated in a day."

Tracy shook her head. "That's what I'm afraid of."

Mrs. Allen put her head back in the door. "Come on. That

boy needs to pay for deceiving us. We are going to King's BBQ, and I'm ordering ribs."

Tracy grabbed her purse, turned out the lights and locked the door. "I like your mom's style." She pinched Mika's arm again.

"Hey, stop that."

Tracy rolled her eyes. "Like that hurt. I can't get enough skin between my fingers to twist that pinch."

"That has nothing to do with anything. A pinch is a pinch."

"Oh my stars. Has anyone ever told you, you're a drama queen?"

Mika puffed out his chest. "A king maybe."

The truck horn sounded. Mrs. Allen waved for them to come. He shook his head.

Tracy just kept from grinning. "Follow me home. That way you can drop me off when we are done."

Tracy's eye widened as the waitress set her rib platter in front of her. "There is no way I can eat all of this."

Mrs. Allen smiled. "Take it home. The meat is good cold, and the rest heats up well."

"How long does a takeout plate last you, Mrs. Allen?"

She patted Mika's arm. "This boy packs away the food and usually finishes off what I don't eat. If you don't want to take it all, I will take some. That would be a treat for me." She sighed. "Unless someone eats it all by tomorrow."

Tracy grinned as Mika rolled his eyes.

"Do either of you know what kind of or how many decorations you want?"

"Mika talked about a small tree in my window. There's really not much room for anything else."

Mrs. Allen smiled. "If we could find two trees that looked alike – one for your window and one for Mika's." She waved her hand. "Decorate them with a common theme." She stared at the ceiling. "You both have small items in the store you can use as Christmas ornaments. The hardware store has little screwdrivers and such. Put some lights on the tree and add those small shiny things. It might entice someone to come in and buy."

Mika bumped her leg. "Told you Mom could decorate. The rules don't specify we have to decorate. I vote we let her do it. Between the stuff in our stores and the stuff Mom has, shouldn't cost anything but the tree."

"And if your mom doesn't want to?"

"Oh, dear. I'll be glad to help. My house has been decorated since Thanksgiving, and this will give me something to do."

"I would really appreciate it, Mrs. Allen, since I'm not much of a decorator. Plus, I doubt Mika will leave me in peace until I agree."

Mika rubbed his hands together. "Let's eat so we can get the trees."

Tracy groaned. She couldn't remember the last time she had eaten so much. Bouncing around as the truck hit every pothole in the road didn't help. "Slow down."

Mika shook his head. "It's worse going slower. Trust me."

They slid to a stop in front of the tree lot. Tracy jumped out of the truck and leaned over with her hands on her knees.

Mika put his hand on her back. "You okay?"

She took several deep breaths then slowly stood. "Too much food, too much bouncing. Does that thing have shocks?"

Mika laughed. "Of course, but they quit working ages ago."

Mrs. Allen stepped out of the truck. "It's much worse in the back seat. I try to never ride in this thing."

"Alright you two, it's not that bad."

Mrs. Allen rolled her eyes. "Just be thankful you don't have to ride to Dumas in it. You really don't want to experience that."

Jacob Tanner strolled out to the truck. "How are you folks tonight?"

"Mr. Tanner, The ladies are talking bad about my truck. You've used it before."

Mr. Tanner nodded. "I did, and I'll tell anyone that will listen, it was a miracle I made it home." He shook his head. "Can't believe it still runs."

"That's enough bad-mouthing my truck. It does everything I ask it to." Mika crossed his arms over his chest. "Including hauling bags and bags of gravel and dirt for someone who shall remain nameless. Tonight it's gonna haul Christmas trees."

Mrs. Allen laughed. "Jacob, we need two trees about three and a half feet tall. Slim so they'll fit in store windows."

"I should have some like that in the back. Good thing you want small ones. Most of the big ones are gone."

Mrs. Allen pointed at them. "You two wander while Jacob and I go tree hunting."

Tracy smiled as Mrs. Allen and Jacob Tanner headed for the back of the lot. "You weren't joking about your mom and Christmas."

"She'll enjoy helping us. She's already helped everybody in town decorate their store or home, or bake cookies, or wrap presents. She shops early and every present is wrapped and every inch of the house is decorated the week after Thanksgiving. "

Tracy sighed. "I can handle the small stuff but large is beyond me."

"Folks won't expect us to have Christmas decorations in every inch of our stores since neither one of us sells foofoo."

"Foofoo?"

Mika nodded. "You know candles, cards, lotions, and knick-knacks – foofoo. I've been to a few of those stores hunting Mom's present, and there's hardly enough room to navigate much less find something to buy." He waved his hand at one of the walkways. "It may take Mom a while to find what she wants. We might as well look around."

Tracey blew on her coffee, and wondered why she let Mika badger her into getting a tree for her house. She cocked her head. The tree did list to one side and one side didn't have many branches on it so shoving it in a corner would look the best, but. . . If she put it up, other people needed to see it. So, it would go in the front window. No one but her would see the bad side. She grinned. Maybe Mrs. Allen could fix that part.

Tracey frowned. Her grandparents had always decorated. There might be ornaments in the attic. She remembered the attic as big and dark with junk everywhere. The walls seemed to creak and groan. She shivered. She might do a little badgering of her own because she was not going up there by herself.

Tracey refilled her coffee mug, picked up her thermos and headed out. She didn't know what time Mrs. Allen would show up but she needed to have the window cleaned out before she opened the shop.

She pulled in front of Mika's truck and stopped. Lazy snowflakes drifted from the sky. She sighed. The first snow fall of the season, and she hoped it just dusted the ground and melted. The front door tended to stick during cold wet weather. If Mrs. Allen made many trips in and out, they might have to prop it open. She started to put the key in the door when Mika walked out of the back of his shop.

"Morning."

Tracy smiled. "Morning."

"I was about to get my tree. Let's get yours inside."

"Okay. I still need to clean out a place in the window for it. Just set it in the middle of the floor." Tracey opened the door, and Mika carried the tree in.

"Steve's working today so one of us can help Mom with the decorations. Seriously, my mom's a little over-the-top..." he set the tree down, "...about everything, not just Christmas. She won't be offended if you ask her to tone down the decorations."

"That's good to know."

Mika winked. "And if things get too out of hand, call me. I might be able to help. She just understands how important this contest is."

"Thanks. I'll keep that in mind."

He stopped at the back door. "Coffee's made if you want some."

Tracey held up her mug. "Taken care of."

"Now that's a mug of coffee."

She held up her thermos. "All day coffee drinker."

Mika nodded. "So am I."

Tracey frowned. Actually seeing the sheen of dust on the window and the dust bunnies stacked up in the corners shocked her. After this, checking into a professional cleaning company topped her list.

She looked at her watch and frowned. The store opened in five minutes. Picking up the supplies, she headed to the washroom, soaped her arms down, splashed cold water in her face, and tied her hair back with a bandana.

She unlocked the door and flipped the open sign over. Four or five customers a week meant a good week for her. The bell over the door jangled before she got back to her work counter.

"Hello, dear."

"Mrs. Allen, you're early."

"Unexpected trip to Amarillo this afternoon. Since we know how we're going to decorate the trees, it's mainly deciding what to put on them. Mika and Steve are putting up the lights around his window. When they are through, Mika will come over here to put up yours."

"But I—"

"Don't worry about a thing. I brought lights and other stuff with me. I'll just look around to see what we can use for ornaments."

The bell jingled again and Mika walked in a rope of lights on his arm. "My lights are up. If you'll just go stand in the store in case someone comes in, and send Steve over, we'll have your lights up in no time."

Tracey frowned.

Mrs. Allen smiled. "Go ahead, dear. The quicker we get everything done, the quicker we can go away and leave you alone."

"But I –"

Mrs. Allen patted her arm. "It's okay. Mika told me you don't like a lot of people fussing around you."

Tracey's eyebrows shot up. "What?"

Mika put his arm around her shoulder and walked her to the door. "Won't take ten minutes. Don't expect a customer this early. If somebody comes in, nod and smile and point them in the right direction."

She scowled. "We need to talk."

"Later." He pushed her out the door and shut it.

She glared at him through the window then chopped at her own throat. He laughed and turned away. She strode next door, yanked the door open stepped in, and slammed it so hard the bell above the door almost flipped of its hook. "He thinks I'm joking."

Steve's eyes widened.

"Oh, don't worry, I won't bite but I am mad enough to spit nails."

Steve got as close to the wall as he could.

"Tell your boss I'll be armed and dangerous when he gets back."

Steve nodded, and hurried out the door.

She yanked the door open. "And I know where the nails are."

"Are you alright, dear?"

Tracey blinked and looked right. "Good morning, Mrs. Enis." She opened the door and ushered Mrs. Enis in. "What are you doing here so early?"

"I come in early on Friday and pick up a sack of fresh dog bedding for Bugger. It should be behind the counter. Mika always has it ready for me."

Tracey walked around the counter and there sat a large sack of woodchips. Since Bugger might weigh ten pounds and rarely stayed outside—. "There is a large bag here. Is that what you get?"

"Oh yes, dear. I completely cover the Bugger's outside area pen." Mrs. Enis sat her purse on the counter and counted out some money. "I hate to ask but can you put the sack in the car? Mika or Steve always does. My son will get it out when I get home."

"Of course." Tracey picked up the sack.

Back in the store, she counted the money – three dollars and forty-five cents. The bag easily sold for six or more dollars.

The bell jingled, and Mika walked in. She held up the three dollars.

Mika grinned. "You made a sale?"

"Mrs. Enis."

"Oh-h-h. I forgot it's Friday."

"Do you even sell woodchips?"

"Yes. And gravel, and mulch, and sand."

"That bag of woodchips looked well used. How long have you been selling her the same bag for three dollars and forty-five cents?"

He chuckled. "Unless the bag is in really bad shape or Ricky, her son, used it filling Bugger's space, he'll bring it back tomorrow, pick up the money, and slide it into his mom's purse when she's not looking so she'll have exactly three dollars and forty- five cents to pay with. If he needs a new bag, he'll come in, pay for the sack and pick up the three dollars and forty-five cents."

"Is there something wrong with her?"

"Not a thing. Mentally, she's sharp as a tack. Ricky works hard to slide a few things past her–like the woodchips. She still sees good. Is a careful driver."

"I'm surprised she still drives."

"She quit driving to Amarillo years ago. Ricky or Mable, her granddaughter, take her to Dumas. But, she drives into Buzbee a couple times a week. Everybody knows that orange 1970s VW Beatle with the big yellow flowers and bright blue peace sign."

"I've been stuck behind it a few times."

"Next time park your car, trot up to her window, and ask her to pull over. She will. If you ask her to let you drive the Beatle, she will."

"How do you know that?"

"I've done it. I park it wherever she's going then walk back to my truck." Mika smiled. "Or ask about Bugger. She'll talk about him, and it gives the other cars time to pass. They always wave but they're waving at Mrs. Enis not you, and she always waves back."

"You really do that?"

Mika nodded. "I'm not the only one. Everybody in town takes care of Mrs. Enis."

Tracey crossed her arms. "This doesn't let you off for shoving me out of my own shop and basically telling me to get lost."

"That reminds me. Steve wouldn't have the slightest idea how to help your customers." He opened the door and motioned her out.

She frowned at him. "You're doing it again."

"Yep."

In her head, Tracey dared Mika to come in. She had managed to act nice while Mrs. Allen and Steve worked on her shop but inside she seethed. That man had no right to treat her so cavalier.

Ida Folley stopped out front and studied the window. She

looked at it from all angles then walked in. She glanced all around. "Nice."

"I'm glad you like it. Mrs. Allen decided on the theme and decorated."

Ida smiled. "She's decorated most of the windows in town."

"Have you looked at Mika's window yet?"

"I have." She shrugged. "Being on the contest committee, I kind of have to. I do like the simplicity of your decorations. And they fit the shop." She walked over to the tree. "Who thought to use keychains and pepper spray as ornaments?"

"Mrs. Allen. She thought the small item theme worked for both stores."

Ida nodded. "It does." She wondered over to the shelves. "Tracey, do you have any idea what Walter would want for Christmas? We always do one present, set price. The tools he needs are above my budget. I know he comes in here a lot. If I didn't know my Walter so well, I might think you are the reason." She grinned. "As cute as you are."

Tracey felt the red creeping up her neck.

Ida laughed. "Is there anything he has his eye on but won't buy?"

Tracey reached under the counter and pulled out a box. She opened it and showed Ida the holster inside. "He looks at it every time he comes in. I keep it under the counter so no one else can buy it. He'll talk himself into it one day."

"How much?"

"One hundred. It's a good holster and will last a long time."

"I'll take it."

"Do you want me to stamp Walter's initials on it?"

"How long will it take?"

"You can pick it up Monday."

"Do it then."

"Mrs. Folley, may I ask a nosey question?"

"Sure. I might say 'no comment' but you're free to ask."

"Most of the people I know spend so much money buying

gifts it takes them six months to pay it off. But you and Walter give each other one gift with a price limit. Why?"

"We used to be caught up in that bigger, better frenzy." She shook her head. "All that running around trying to find each item on every person list puts too much stress on the family." Ida swiped her card and signed the receipt. "Actually, we were studying the life of Jesus, and it dawned on us the one best gift God gave was the birth of His son. We decided to emulate Him by giving just one nice gift to the people we love. We taught our children that, and now they are teaching my lovely grandkids."

Tracey followed her to the door, flipped the closed sign and locked it. That was a good explanation. She really looked at the shop. The decorations did suit it. They suited her. She started to unplug the lights in the window and on the tree then stopped. Theirs was the last block on this street. Most people wouldn't walk to here but maybe if the twinkling lights were on they would.

She gathered her stuff and went out the back door. Mika leaned against his truck. She raised her eyebrows. He walked over, opened her door so she could put her stuff in.

"Why are you still here?"

He sighed. "You said we needed to talk. Want to grab a burger or something?"

"I've ordered chicken." She smiled. "Perfect payback."

"Chicken? I like chicken."

"No. You get to go up in the attic and retrieve the Christmas decorations for that tree you badgered me into getting."

"Free food, Christmas decorations, and an evening with a cutie-patootie. I call that fun not payback."

Tracey snorted. "It's definitely payback. You haven't seen the attic."

Tracey looked at the pile of chicken bones, and the bottom of the empty salad bowl. "Did you get enough?"

Mika leaned back and patted his tummy. "I'm comfortably full."

"Good. I can scrounge some ice cream for dessert but that's pretty much it. Tomorrow is grocery shopping day."

"Can I stretch out on the couch and let my food settle?"

"No, you're attic bound."

Mika stood and hitched up his pants. "Okay, let's get it done." He pulled the attic ladder down and motioned her up.

"You're going up first. Payback, remember?"

"The attic is that scary?"

"To a six-year-old, yes."

Mika laughed. "I guess it would be."

She handed him a flashlight.

"Is there a light up here?"

"Single bulb with a pull string in the middle of the room."

"Not coming on."

"I'll get a new bulb." When Tracey reached the top of the ladder, light bounced around the attic.

"How long's it been since anyone's been up here?"

She flipped on her flashlight and moved toward him. "At least ten years."

"No wonder you sent me up here first. You have any idea where the Christmas decorations are?"

"Grammy labeled everything. They shouldn't be too hard to find."

She handed him the bulb. He screwed it in and pulled the string. The light came on, and her eyes widened. It didn't throw much light in the room but since he was standing right under it, it highlighted the large spider on his head. "Be still."

He posed. "Is it showing me to my best advantage?"

She shook her head. "Not you. The spider in your hair."

"WHAT!" He froze.

"It's not hairy-scary just long-legged."

20

"I don't care what kind it is. Kill it."

Tracey grabbed an old magazine from a stack of them, rolled it up and started to thwack him on the head.

He put out his hands, panic in his eyes. "Don't smash it. That won't kill it. It will just burrow down into my hair and bite me then you'll be racing me to the ER in Dumas. Sweep sideways and knock it OFF."

"Bend over."

He did, and she knocked it off. When it hit the floor, he stomped it then ground it into the boards.

"Are you okay?"

He straightened and headed toward the ladder. "I'm fine but since this is obviously a den of spiders, I won't be back up here till pest control has been here. I'll go shopping with you tomorrow for Christmas decorations."

"But—"

He held up his hand. "Sorry, but I'm done for the night. Let me know when you're ready to head to Dumas tomorrow."

Tracey stopped him at the front door with a hand on his arm. "Mika, are you really that scared of spiders?"

His whole body shivered. "Screaming like a little girl, scared."

Who knew such a big tough guy could be scared of spiders. She bit her lip to keep from laughing. "Do you need a hug?"

"Yes."

When she put her arms around him, he picked her up, and held her close. The word fierce came to mind. It wasn't too tight. It didn't hurt. It was just—fierce. He set her down and walked out the door.

Tracey locked the door and flipped the sign to closed. Traffic had been heavy this morning. Maybe Mrs. Allen was right about the lights and tree. Several customers had bought stuff off the tree when they realized it was for sale. All morning during the lulls, she replaced the ornaments. Some of the keychains had sold out completely.

After locking her back door, she strolled by the big four-wheel drive diesel crew cab truck idling behind the hardware store. She had never seen it before. When she banged on the back door of the hardware store, Steve poked his head out.

"You ready?"

She nodded.

Steve pushed a button on a fob and the truck's doors unlocked. "Mr. Allen said to give him a few minutes. Feel free to wait inside the truck." He paused. "Unless you need to come in the store."

"I'm good out here."

Tracey wondered how she was supposed to climb into the cab. Short legs meant she'd have to jump. She opened the door and moved back as a step slid out. She climbed in, rolled down the window, closed the door and watched the step slid back in. Fancy.

Hot air filled the cab. She looked but wasn't willing to push any buttons, so she rolled up her window. The heated seat felt good on her back. She relaxed against it, found the button to lean it back and closed her eyes. "I could get use to this."

The driver's door opened, and the truck dipped as Mika climbed in.

"What do you—"

She held up her hand. "Some kind of burger. No talking. I may sleep until we get to Dumas." She fastened her seatbelt and snuggled deeper into the seat. The truck started moving, the heater subsided to a light breeze. "Nice."

"Hey, wake up."

Tracey opened her eyes. They were in the parking lot of the

big box store in Dumas. She sat her seat up. "I slept all the way here? Did I miss the food?"

"You starving? We can grab something after you finish shopping. "

Tracey shrugged. "Works for me."

"You have a long list?"

"Nope. Only come to Dumas when I have large items to get – like washing powder, toilet paper. Today is the day. I'd rather pay a little more for most items in Buzbee, so I don't have to make this trip." She chuckled. "I only go to Amarillo when Mom summons me."

When they got inside, she picked up a small bag of chips and a cold drink. "You need something to tide you over?"

Mika looked a little sheepish. "No. I stopped at the Dairy Freeze and got a burger. You were snoring by then, so I didn't wake you."

She punched his arm. "I do not snore."

"Gently, but. . ." He grinned, ". . .you snore. You want me to help shop or get lost?"

"Get lost. Two hours should satisfy my wander lust. Where do you want to meet?"

"The Christmas section."

She opened her chips, gave him a thumbs-up sign, and walked off.

Tracey picked up a slice of pizza and sat on the couch.

"Do we want—"

"No."

"What if we—"

"Nope."

"But there's just so much open space on this side. We could—"

"Nadda. I like it just like it is."

Mika crossed his arms. "Seriously?"

"Yep."

He backed up to the couch. "But it's just so—"

"Perfect."

He tilted his head, a look of doubt on his face. "You really think so?"

"I do."

He took a bite of pizza as he studied the tree. The part facing the window looked good, but the part facing the living room had big gaps. "Wonder what chewed up this side."

"Doesn't matter."

Mika snorted. "You knew it would still be on the lot the day after Christmas and felt sorry for it." He shook his head. "It's your tree. You're happy, I'm happy."

"I'm. . .content with my first in-my-own-house Christmas tree." She patted the couch. "Sit."

Mika sat on the edge of the couch, leaned back and stretched his feet out in front of him. "This is a comfy couch."

Tracey raised an eyebrow. "Don't get too comfy. I have questions."

"Mine first." Mika closed his eyes. "What turned you off Christmas? I remember you enjoyed Christmas with your grandparents when we were kids."

"Things were simpler then." Tracey pulled her knees up under her chin. "I got tired of anxious people franticly rushing to get everything done perfectly, so that the people – who are supposed to be their friends – approved of who they pretended to be instead of who they are. Watching them go into debt just to satisfy a selfish person's desire to have everything. Rude people pushing and shoving to get an item before it runs out." Tracey waved her hand. "The whole fake retail Christmas thing."

"Not going to argue. But we can't let how other people act at Christmas dictate how we celebrate, can we?"

Tracey scowled at him.

Mika grinned. "What?"

She stood, closed the lid on the pizza box and handed it to him. "Take this home." She walked to the door, opened it and motioned for him to leave.

He stopped beside her. "I thought you had questions."

"You pretty much answered them." She gently pushed him out the door. "I was okay with being bah-humbug at Christmas until you opened your mouth and nixed it with your – we can't let how other people act – statement."

"But I—"

"'Night Mika."

She waited until he had turned the corner toward his house then closed the door. She didn't remember ever hearing anyone explain the things they did at Christmas. The star or angel on top of the tree was obvious but what about the tree itself or the lights on the tree.

After getting more tea, she sat at her desk, opened her search engine and typed in Christmas tree. It showed pages of different types of tree and how to buy them. She tried 'what does the Christmas tree symbolize'. She read the lines under each article headline and opened a few to read them.

She refilled her glass of tea then walked over to her tree and lightly brushed the branches. "Who knew you meant so much to so many different cultures."

Two hours later she rubbed her eyes and shut down the search engine. "There are so many different reasons people put up trees and lights and garland and stars and — But why do would I do it?"

She got her Bible, sat on the couch, opened to Luke and started reading.

Tracey slid into the pew by Mrs. Allen and nodded at Mika. They sang three songs and prayed. It was the first Sunday in December, and Pastor Roberts began his series on Luke. She pulled out her iPad and started taking notes.

"Please stand for the dismissal prayer."

Surprised, Tracey looked up then bowed her head as Pastor Roberts prayed. She put up her iPad and stepped into the aisle.

Mrs. Allen stopped her. "Tracey, we're having a burger at the Dairy Freeze. Would you like to come?"

"I will if you allow me to buy. I owe you something for decorating my store."

"Decorating your store was fun." Mrs. Allen smiled. "But I never turn down free food. Ride with us?"

When they had ordered, Mika led them to a booth.

"Mika, did you just order one burger and fry?"

He nodded. "Mom always gives me half of her burger." He smiled. "And I was hoping you'd do the same."

"Fat chance."

When Mika put her food in front of her, she changed her mind. "I didn't think about this chili burger being regular size. I usually order a junior burger. Give me that plate. I might as well give you half of this thing now." After giving him half her burger, she said, "Mrs. Allen, I received a lot of compliments on my tree Saturday. I sold out of the old red truck keychain. People were buying them as Christmas ornaments. I pulled up the website I buy from, and they even had one with a Christmas tree in the back. I'm going to have a lot of different kinds on hand next year."

Mrs. Allen pursed her lips. "I might put up a small tree next year with nothing but those red trucks as ornaments."

"Tracey, would you like to walk back to your car? I haven't looked at any of the other store windows. We could scope out the competition."

"Sure."

"Mom." He tossed her his keys. "We're walking back."

Mrs. Allen hugged Tracey. "Thank you for lunch." She climbed in the truck and drove off.

Mika flipped the collar of his coat up and put his hands in his pocket. "Mind if I ask another question?"

"It's according to the question."

"Since you threw me out last night, I was wondering if you got your thinking done."

Tracey put her hands on her hips. "I did not throw you out. I merely escorted you to the door."

"Okay, you gently threw me out."

"After three hours of internet research and reading Luke – yeah. I understand why people celebrate Christmas the way they do. Even those who aren't particularly religious."

"What did you decide?"

"That you're right. And you don't know how much it pains me to say that..."

Mika laughed.

"...But I can't let the way other people act dictate the way I celebrate Christmas. I know my celebrating will be low key. That's how I live my life. It's the reason I moved to Buzbee. Why did you move back?"

"Basically, the same. Buzbee is very layed back. Plus I want to be a fixture in Mom's life by the time she needs help. Like Ricky and Mrs. Enis." He stopped in front of a window. "Too much, right?"

"Definitely."

They passed several more decked out windows, glanced at one another, shook their heads, and kept walking.

Tracey put her hands in her coat pocket. "Mind if I ask a nosey finical question?"

"It's according to the question."

"You drive an old beat-up truck everyday then Saturday you show up in a brand-spanking new one loaded with bells and whistles. I know how much I make at my store. I'm sure you make more but closer to the beat up truck than the bells and whistles."

"I own a real estate firm in Amarillo. I have good people working for me now and most of my work is online. I go to Amarillo once every two weeks. I'm training Steve to run the store, so if I decide to take time off, I can." Mika pulled her to a stop in front of one of the windows. He tilted his head and scrunched his face. "What were they thinking?"

Tracey shrugged.

He grabbed her hand and started walking again. "Anyway, I paid cash for the bells and whistles. It put a dent in my savings, but I'm not paying a big truck note or high interest rates. What about you? You're a gunsmith and moved to a town with a population of about three thousand people."

"I do most of my business through my online store. But my reputation is growing..." She paused. "...And believe it or not, I think the Christmas decoration contest is helping. Two men dropped off their revolvers to be worked on. Said they saw our window decorations on the news and looked me up online."

They reached her car.

"You got room in that thing for me?"

Tracey smiled. "Maybe if you push the seat all the way back and hang your legs out the window."

"If you drive like Mrs. Enis, I can trot by the car."

She poked him in the chest. "Get in."

Even with the seat all the way back, his knees were under his chin. "When we go places," Mika cut his eyes at her, "we're going in my truck. Unless you decide to buy a much bigger vehicle."

Tracey pulled into Mika's driveway. She turned toward him. "You expect us to go places now that the decorations are up?"

"Of course." He opened the car door but didn't move. "You may have to push me out."

She put her hands on his shoulder and shoved.

"Ouch, wait. That's not going to work. Come around and pull."

Tracey walked around. He held out his arm. She grabbed it and started pulling. He leaned out the door but didn't get out of the seat. She started laughing so hard, she sat down.

Mika crawled out on his hands and knees then sat down beside her. He bumped her shoulder. "Want to know why the great Buzbee Christmas contest is important to me?"

"Sure."

"Did you know I had a crush on you when we were teenagers?"

Surprised, Tracey frowned. "No. You were part of the football crowd, dating cheerleaders, that kind of stuff. I spent my days in martial art classes, and learning how to work on guns with my grandfather."

"Believe it or not, you intimidated me back then."

"But you've always been a large, take-charge guy."

"Not when it came to you." He shrugged. "I like you, Tracey. A lot. Over this past year, I've tried to ask you out several times but you ignored me."

"I did—"

He placed a finger on her lips. "This contest gave me the excuse to make you spend time with me. See, I know you have a soft heart and wouldn't outright refuse to help me win this contest." He chuckled. "Being your landlord didn't hurt." Mika leaned in and gently kissed her. "I want to spend years of more time with you. Think you might like that?"

Tracey could still fell his kiss on her lips. "I might."

Mika leaned back and smiled. "One more question. That day

I came into the store, and you had a real smile on your face —why?"

"I was thinking about throat-punching the next person who walked in the door and said Merry Christmas." She shrugged. "It was you."

A Family Christmas

By:
Diann Floyd Boehm

Author Diann Floyd Boehm

Diann Floyd Boehm is a former classroom teacher and an award-winning international author. Diann writes children's books and young adult historical fiction books., Diann' books are designed to inspire her readers to be kind, love themselves, and to "Embrace Imagination." You can find all her books on Amazon.

Diann's Story Garden YouTube Channel gives children the opportunity to hear different children authors read their stories a well as Diann read her own stories.

Diann does speaking engagements, book signings as well as author visitations. Her creative flair encompasses the performing arts and performing in musical theatre productions in Dubai produced by Popular Productions out of the UK. In addition, Diann enjoys making guest appearances on various live streaming shows. Diann is the cohost with Dr. Jacalyn on her USA Global TV and Radio™®. Diann continues to be involved in various humanitarian projects with multiple organizations.

Diann was born to parents of George and Mabel Floyd in Tulsa, Oklahoma, but grew up in Texas with five brothers. She has traveled extensively to many parts of the world and has lived in the Philippines and Dubai.

Keep in touch with Diann by joining her newsletter: www.Diannfloydboehm.com

A Family Christmas

ॐ

My five brothers and I piled into our green Mercury station wagon along with my parents and went to pick out the perfect Christmas tree. It was December 1964, and I was 10 years old.

All of the kids were excited, even my older brother, who tried to play it cool. But when we drove up to the Christmas tree lot, he couldn't help but let go of his teenager ways and join in the fun as we started walking among all the trees of various sizes. Some trees were even flocked! The Christmas tree growers were all about making it a family experience. They wanted kids to enjoy the magic they created with their Christmas tent full of trees. There was merriment around us, with carolers in period costumes singing familiar Christmas songs. There were free cups of hot chocolate for us to enjoy as we began searching on the cold, clear December night.

I remember being surrounded by the smell of Christmas trees, and my brothers and I thought it would be lovely to smell Christmas all year 'round. What a feeling of joy and happiness, mainly because we all got along, which meant no fighting – of course, my two baby brothers were too little to cause problems. I would hear various trees' names: Blue Spruce, Douglas Fir, and

Noble Fir. Finally, my mom would find a tree and then Dad would remind her it was too tall, so we'd all continue looking and looking. I think my parents had a game of their own to keep hunting for the perfect tree so the experience would last a little longer. My mom was all about creating memories. When my parents finally agreed on the ideal tree, the salesman tied it on top of the wagon, and we sang Christmas carols all the way home.

Dad would set up the tree, which I don't think was an easy task. My two older brothers, James and Danny, would hold it while Dad placed it on the stand. Then my momma would say, "It's leaning to the left," or "It's leaning to the right." Then, when Dad thought she was happy, Momma would say, "I think we need to turn it, so the fuller side is facing us when we sit on the sofa." Dad would get up off the floor and take the tree out of the holder. My brothers would help get the tree in the stand, then Dad would hear Momma say, "Perfect." Then carefully, one at a time, one brother would get up, Dad would make his way to the floor, and my other brother would help hold the tree. Momma would be watching as Dad would screw the long screws into the tree for balance. Then Momma poured her usual sugar water into the stand.

The whole family would stand back and look at this tall, fat Christmas tree in the corner of the living room. Then, of course, we'd have to wait until the next night for decorating, but Momma made it worth it.

The whole family was anxious to decorate the tree. Saturday could not come fast enough because it was dedicated to the Christmas tree festivities. First, Momma and Dad brought the Christmas ornaments down from the attic. Then some of my brothers and I helped Momma make Christmas cookies to eat when it was time to decorate the tree.

The cookies were always extra special because Momma would get out Great-grandma's sugar cookie recipe. Momma was brilliant ... she had some tricks up her sleeve to keep us engaged in the activity. Unfortunately, I didn't learn to appreciate what Momma was doing until I was older. She had the dough already made and hard so that we could press the cookie cutter into the dough we were given and put it on the cookie sheet. She had some cookies baked and ready to be decorated while the others were cooking. Momma knew that was our favorite part. We each had our own colored icing and dough, so we wouldn't fight and it'd be fair.

You would have thought Momma was a schoolteacher; those are just Momma tricks to keep kids from fighting and saying, "He has more dough than me." Or "Danny won't share!" When I think back, I sometimes tear up, wishing I could tell Momma just how much I love those memories.

While some of us were inside making cookies, James and Danny were outside with our dad. My dad would be on a ladder, and one brother would hold the ladder steady while the other one made sure the Christmas outdoor lights didn't get tangled while handing them each time our dad would say, "Give me more" as he made his way around the trim of the house. Dad would outline the whole house in huge multi-color lights. When my brothers and dad were all finished, my dad would take a break, but Mom wouldn't let him do it for long. Why? Because it was time to string the Christmas lights on the tree so the tree would be ready to decorate in the evening.

The kids were sent out to play until dinner time, which was OK with us; we wanted to see what our friends were up to. But, of course, some of our friends were basically up to the same thing. Their parents were either decorating outside the house, getting the tree, or about to decorate the tree. It felt like the whole neighborhood was filled with joy. There wasn't one family in some way or another not getting ready for Christmas.

I went down the street to my best friend Anna's house. Anna had five sisters and one brother; it was fun at her house as something was always going on. Anna's momma was like my momma ... she had lots of kids and was a working mom. I remember Mrs. Rhodes. No matter how tired she was, she always smiled and never minded setting a plate at the dinner table for her children's friends. So when I arrived at Anna's house, I was so excited, as Anna said, "Great, Theresa, you are here! Come inside." Her momma got out her Elvis Presley's Christmas album, and Sherry (her sister) and I ate and pretended to sing with Elvis and entertain the little sisters.

Of course, Anna had said the magic words: "Elvis" and "singing." My Aunt Jane was always playing Elvis when I would stay with her. My aunt had a big crush on the singer, so I did too. Elvis might have been older, but I loved to dance to his music.

Anna knew I loved Elvis, so I gave a huge smile and started having fun. Anna and I would pretend we were holding microphones and sing "Blue Christmas," and of course, Anna's little sisters wanted us to sing "Here Comes Santa Claus" over and over. Then, just when it seemed we were having fun, Momma would call for me to come home. Usually, I'd say, "I don't want to," and make a fuss, but I knew what it meant in this case. So, home I went with a big smile singing "Will have a Blue, Blue, Blue Christmas" over and over. I loved the song's ending, even though I didn't understand what it meant at the time. I just liked how Elvis sang the words.

When I was making my way home, I spotted my older brothers leaving their friends' homes and we all walked inside together. Momma had us wash up for dinner. I think that was the fastest my brothers and I finished our meal. There was no fighting, just eye contact to hurry up. Dad was grinning because he knew we wanted the family fun to begin. Momma tried to slow you down, but it was a hopeless cause. We were ready for the family fun to begin. Momma brought out the Christmas cookies and started playing Christmas records as the decorating began. We each had our own box of ornaments as we received a new Christmas decoration from Santa.

My ornaments were always angels, so there was no confusion about which ones were mine. My brothers' ornaments had a Santa that was playing football or Santa playing baseball as well as other sports. Momma would mark their initials on them to be sure they didn't get confused on which ornament was theirs. Sometimes I wanted to trade an angel for a Santa, but Momma said, "No trading allowed. Santa gave those to you, and you would not want to disappoint him." So that put an end to anyone trading.

It was always special to unwrap an ornament. It was like you had a brand new decoration since you hadn't seen it for a whole year. It was as if you were looking at an old friend who had been waiting all year for this day to come.

I wish you could've seen the different ornaments; some shined because they were made of glass and painted beautifully. Each time we unwrapped one, we'd show it to each other, and Momma would give us a Christmas hanger to hang the ornament from a tree branch. Of course, we all wanted ours to be in the front of the tree, but Momma had a way of making sure some made it to the back of the tree to be seen outside, even though we knew you couldn't see them. Since the number of ornaments reflected our age, it made it tough for my little brothers because they only had one or two ornaments at the time. So we would take turns letting the little ones put up one of our ornaments. Momma and Daddy had plenty of glass balls in Christmas colors, red, blue, and green, to help make things even. We were excited when the decorations were up because we knew what came next.

My big brother seemed to be bored with it all, and I guess my dad sensed it. So, this year my dad let him put the star on the tree. You should've seen my big brother's face when my dad said, "James, where do you think you're going? Come back here." My brother looked very disgusted, and I could tell he was back in what my parents called "the teenager mood." Dad said, "James, it's time to pass the torch, so from this Christmas forward, you'll be in charge of placing the Christmas Star on the tree."

My brother questioned, "Me?"

"Yes, and you and your Momma and I are making it extra special." We all looked at Momma, wondering what it could be. Momma handed James a medium-sized box, and my brother opened it. It was the most beautiful star I'd ever seen for a Christmas tree. We all said, "Wow," at the same time.

James pulled it out of the box, and it had a wire hanging down, and that's when we all realized that it lit up. So, again we all said in unison, "Wow." James looked at my momma and dad and smiled. My dad motioned for him to get on the ladder that he'd placed close enough to the tree to reach the top. My big brother was already very tall, so it would not be a problem for him. James climbed on the ladder while my dad and Danny held it and he carefully placed the star on top of the tree. Momma told everyone to stand back and asked James to plug in the star.

We all stood back looking at the tree, and even James was grinning from ear to ear as the Christmas magic returned to him, and he was finally ready to be with us. Believe it or not, Momma and Dad had two more things left. The first was that each of us was given four candy canes to place on the tree. Each cane represented a Sunday in Advent! When you have five siblings and two parents, that made for lots of candy canes – 32 to be exact. Hunting for a particular spot on the tree was an adventure on its own. Sometimes my brothers and I would want the same branch for our candy cane, but somehow, we managed to figure out a way not to fight. The candy canes seemed to make the tree more exciting, or maybe it was because we knew we would get one on Sunday. Once we found a spot for all our candy canes, Momma gave each of us tinsel to throw on the tree. Momma would tell us the story of how much she loved candy canes and tinsel on her Christmas tree when she was little and that every tree should be covered in tinsel and have candy canes.

When we finally finished decorating the tree, we all stepped back to see the whole tree, as my dad plugged in the lights. I remember all of the kids simultaneously saying, "Wow!" at the various colored lights, the tinsel twinkling just like snow. The ornaments hanging from the branches and the candy canes added extra merriment to the tree. I remember looking at the star and glancing over at James, and much to my surprise, he was smiling and staring at the Christmas Star he had put up for the first time. I've never seen my brother look so peaceful as he continued to look at the lighted star. I looked back up at the tree and realized it was a spectacular moment as each of us smiled at each other, and the feeling of joy filled the room. Momma and Dad were arm and arm, my little brothers were giggling, and the rest of us were just looking at that fat Christmas tree whose branches reached the TV, but luckily not the rabbit ears on the TV. Then the best thing ever was when we all went outside and saw the lights on the house shining brightly. We stood in the yard admiring our Christmas tree glowing in the picture window.

Then James said, "Look, you can even see the Christmas Star!"

I remember Dad saying, "Yes, you can; you did great James."

We looked around, and other families were out in their yard admiring their tree too. We all waved or yelled Christmas cheer before going inside. I remember thinking, "*Oh, what a night.*" We happily went to bed with our hearts filled with joy.

Now you would think the story would be over, but oh no. My brothers and I would watch for the Sears and Montgomery Wards catalogs and mark all the things we wished for. Those catalogs were the secret to possible dreams coming true, as every toy and doll one could imagine were in those pages! Momma collected green stamps, so we had the green stamp catalog too. My grandma and Aunt Jane would even have green stamps and give them to us to place in Momma's books, and we were excited. We couldn't wait till Momma had enough green stamps to fill a book, and of course, we all had suggestions on how she could spend her green stamps.

Do you remember saying to your parents, "Is it almost time for Christmas? When is Christmas going to be here?" If not, well, they were popular questions in our household. I think that's why Momma had the candy canes, to help us remember it is the season of Advent, which meant waiting. Momma had an Advent Wreath at church; each Sunday, she would light a candle at dinner time. Why? Because we knew after we had dinner, it would be Candy Cane Time! We'd talk about presents and how many weeks till Christmas. It was a happy time. Who knew a candy cane could bring so much joy into a home? I think for my parents, it meant peace and quiet for a bit.

The tree became more beautiful each week, and my Momma did something different this year. She decided to give us all Christmas names, and Santa would be the only one to use those names. James was "Honey Bear" because he was always eating honey, especially with peanut butter. There was "Danny Boy" because my momma loved that song and always said she'd have a son named Danny. Jonathon was "Freckles" because he had lots of angel kisses, or at least he was told that's why he had so many freckles. Then there was the "Dimple Dutchman" because David had a dimple, blond hair, and blue eyes. Then there was the "Cuddly Tiger" because my baby brother, Keith, would never be without his tiger stuffed animal, and then, of course, me the "Princess" because I was the only girl. I like to think we were all excited about our names, but truth be told, if my two older brothers were as enthusiastic as the rest of us, they hid it well because that's what older brothers do, especially if they're a teenager.

That year Momma liked my printing, so I was able to address all the Christmas cards. That was extra special. We all signed the Christmas card addressed to our great-grandma, and some of us made pictures for her. Momma always told her how we made the Christmas cookies just like she did with her momma. I remember thinking how special that was when Momma would tell the story each year. She always said it with so much love as she shared a part of her childhood.

As the weeks went by, the tree seemed prettier and prettier, and looking at it outside through the window made it seem even more stunning. The excitement of our neighborhood friends talking about their trees and seeing them when we went to their homes was a feeling of warmth, as all of the kids were anticipating Christmas.

One day, Momma and Dad loaded up the car, and we drove to this neighborhood where Momma said magic took place with their Christmas displays. It took a long time to get there, but it went fast as we sang Christmas carols all the way there. Once we arrived at this particular neighborhood, my brothers and I couldn't get over the size of the houses. We'd never seen homes so gigantic. They were decorated and lit up more than anyone could imagine. We didn't know which side of the street to look at, because each house was glorious. Our necks were turning from one side to the other. All the cars drove very slowly so no one would miss a decoration. Momma was right, the houses were very magical! The homes were covered with tons of lights. Some had a plastic light-up Santa reindeer, while others had angels and a nativity scene—a site to behold.

As we made our way home, my little brothers fell asleep, but the rest of us kept singing. Sometimes Momma would sing a solo of "The Drummer Boy" or Dad would sing a big solo of "White Christmas." My brothers and I would smile at one another because our parents had beautiful voices. It would be the only occasion we'd ever hear our dad sing, and he always winked at Momma during his song. So we had this feeling of contentment and love all around us, and what more could any kids wish for.

Four Sundays passed, and it was Christmas Eve when our whole family went early to my grandma and aunt's home to celebrate Christmas, and goodness was it fun! Then Dad drove us home to prepare for Midnight Mass. Grandma and Aunt Jane always gave us a Christmas outfit and a special gift that somehow, they knew we were hoping for. By the time Christmas Mass was over, we were all ready for bed, and we quickly tucked in so Santa would come. There were never any arguments about bedtime on Christmas Eve, as who would want coal in their stockings after being reasonably good all year?

Morning came and the Christmas candy canes were gone, but

there under the tree, like magic, were more presents than one could imagine. But then again, there were six kids, which makes for a big Christmas. The packages were wrapped carefully with ribbon and bows, and sometimes little decorations were placed by the name tag. We couldn't wait to find our Christmas names. Somehow, they seemed to be buried among my parent's gifts, but when we found them, we'd shout out our Christmas name in awe that Santa knew it and even gave us our wish and a surprise gift! Danny would always say, "Santa is so cool!" Of course, we all agreed as we kept opening gifts. That year I received my first Timex gold watch! I felt very grown-up as I quickly placed the Timex watch around my wrist and told Momma and Daddy the time.

I remember James received a remote-control airplane, which he couldn't wait to get outside and try out. Danny got a new baseball glove which he couldn't wait to break in. I think we played with one another all morning and afternoon, and when James came inside, he played with his baby brothers.

The day before, my momma let me help her make the baby Jesus's birthday cake for the first time and even ice the cake. Then, on Christmas day, Momma worked all afternoon on Christmas dinner with her recipe for honey ham with pineapples and cherries. After that, Dad usually put together bikes or some gadget for one of the boys. It seemed we were busy, and it gave Momma more time to make the special Christmas dinner without us bothering her.

My momma was a hard-working nurse, so she did not spend all day cooking, but when it came to Christmas, let's say it was her favorite time of year to be in the kitchen. Momma would set the dinner table extra pretty with the Advent and Christmas candles. Once the candles were lit, Christmas dinner was served. To top the meal off, we sang "Happy Birthday" to Jesus, and we all blew out the candles together for baby Jesus!

Yes, 1964 was a magical year. I'm not sure where the years went, and now I watch my kids decorate their home and their own Christmas tree. As my kids add their spark to Christmas, I know my Momma and Dad are smiling down from heaven as they see their traditions of tinsels, candy canes on the trees, and even a baby Jesus cake for Christmas day. They see their hard work paid off because they see their grandchildren discovering the true spirit of Christmas: Love.

Lost And Found

By: Terry Korth Fischer

Author Terry Korth Fischer

Terry Korth Fischer writes the Rory Naysmith Mysteries, a cozy-crime series featuring a seasoned city detective relocated to small-town Winterset, Nebraska. Transplanted from the Midwest, Terry lives in Houston, Texas, with her husband and two guard cats. When not writing, she loves reading and basking in sunshine, yet, her heart often wanders to the country's heartland, where she spent a memorable—ordinary but charmed—childhood. Learn more about Terry on her website: https://terrykorthfischer.com

Lost and Found

⌒⌒⌒

After three days on the Lone Star bus, Joyce Hanschu would have welcomed any place that didn't have over-head storage and seatbelts. The Little Rock antique store offered a quiet refuge. The crystal figurines in the display window seemed to beckon her, and the quaint shop looked intriguing and filled with unusual treasures. It also had a coffee bar, which she considered a bonus. The bell over the door jingled when she stepped inside with enthusiasm. Carol, her seatmate, followed.

"I love to browse through old stuff," Carol said, picking up a hand-painted plate. "You'll be surprised to learn I frequent thrift shops back home. People throw away the most interesting things."

Joyce already knew more about Carol than she cared to know. Yet, she had to admit so far, the cheerful widow from Humble had been a pleasant companion. A little too chatty, but it was a long trip from Houston to Atlanta, especially by bus. She never dreamed she'd be traveling alone, not at seventy. But, at least Carol was of her generation and agreeable. She could have done worse.

"Did you notice the figurines in the window?" she asked, noticing a table for two in the coffee bar and heading for it.

Two steps behind, Carol caught her breath. "You don't say? Was it crystal?"

"I don't know, but the pieces looked lovely. I want to check them out, but I'd like a cup of tea first."

"Sure, anything that doesn't come from a dispenser."

Joyce smirked. " 'Convenient stops and ample opportunities to refuel.' I quote the Lone Star brochure."

"Who knew it meant convenience stores and truck stops?"

"The evening meals have been as advertised," said Joyce. "I liked the chuckwagon restaurant in Shreveport last night."

"Today, our whole afternoon is free. No museums or guided tours," said Carol. "I feel like I've been sprung from jail. And tonight, we'll be in Memphis. I can't wait. Graceland!" Her hands covered her heart, right over the glittery snowman's face. "Maybe we'll see an Elvis impersonator."

"I think you can count on it." Joyce flopped her complimentary Lone Star tote onto the table and pulled out a chair. "How long do we have before we need to meet up with the bus? I'm starting to dread the ordeal. Get on. Get off. Get on. Load back up again." Carol looked at her vacantly. Maybe she was complaining too much? "Let's check the itinerary. Do you have one handy?"

Carol nodded, took a seat, and began searching through a kitten-covered canvas bag as she rambled. "Lufkin was okay, but I'd been there before. However, the Christmas light display in Nacogdoches was spectacular."

"I suppose. But I thought it senseless for us to ride another two hours so we could spend the night in Shreveport. Surely, they had Christmas lights in Shreveport? Or hotels in Nacogdoches."

Frowning, Carol pulled out the itinerary. "Didn't you say you liked the restaurant?"

Joyce harrumphed, pulling her copy of the itinerary from the overstuffed bag. She began to study it. "Arrive in Little Rock,

Arkansas, at eleven in the morning after a leisurely breakfast. On your own until boarding the bus at four and enjoying the scenic two-hour trip to Graceland, where you will join the Graceland Christmas Tour at six-thirty." She looked at Carol through squinted eyelids and said flatly, "Another late dinner."

Her companion shrugged, lowering her gaze. "All I said was, I'm looking forward to Memphis."

The waitress took their orders, and they sat with their thoughts, sipping tea from porcelain cups. Carol finally broke their silence, "I take a trip over the Christmas holidays every year. Arthur, bless his heart, passed away five years ago during this time. I dread the thought of sitting at home alone. I also enjoy seeing the seasonal decorations in different parts of the country. Young families, old couples, and newlyweds. It's such fun. Is this your first Christmas trip?"

Joyce squared her shoulders. "I wouldn't be on this Christmas bus tour if April hadn't come up with the bizarre idea for a family Holiday cruise." Carol's eyes widened. Joyce continued anyway. "Then Jeff, *my only son*, went along with the plan, which *only* had room for him and their children." Joyce could feel her face heating up, and lowered her voice. "Their children are my only grandchildren. They are my whole life. So, I ask you, do you think it fair to leave me out at Christmas?"

Carol studied the bottom of her cup and asked, "So, April is your daughter-in-law?"

"Yes." Joyce shook her head with disgust—tight and violent. "I was as mad as all get out when Jeff handed me the ticket. I'm sure it was April's idea. She had the gall to suggest I wouldn't enjoy a child-themed cruise. They were doing me a favor. A Christmas gift from their family to me. So, I don't even have a Christmas gift to look forward to when they return."

"I've heard those cruises can be loud and crowded."

Joyce knew she shouldn't burden Carol with her problems. The season could wear on anyone, and just because her life was upside down, it didn't mean she should ruin her seatmate's holidays. "Let's have something expensive and gooey," she suggested. "It will take our minds off our troubles. Treats on me." She pulled her wallet from the tote and fished a credit card out.

"In that case," said Carol, "I'm fixin' to get one of them marshmallow-topped Santa sundaes. Of course, I don't need three scoops of ice cream, but as you say, we won't be eating anything any time soon." Metallic snowflakes swung from her ears, caught the overhead light, and glistened. Joyce thought their twinkle matched Carol's sweet disposition.

When the sundaes arrived, they dug into the Christmassy delights with relish. Joyce was glad April hadn't sent her to the North Pole or some cold, heartless snowy location. She wasn't home. She wasn't with her grandchildren, but at least she'd made a friend and had the tour to distract her. What could go wrong? She had a full itinerary and hoped the trip would be enjoyable— even without her family.

Licking the last gooey remnant from her spoon, Joyce said, "Look at the time." She signed the credit slip, tucked the credit card back into her wallet, and shoved it into the overfilled bag. "We better get going if we intend to see more of Little Rock." As she stood, the bulging tote toppled, and its contents spilled onto the floor.

"Oh, heavens!" Carol scampered after a loose coin, trapped it underfoot, and then bent to pick it up. "See any more?"

"Jiminy Christmas," Joyce whispered under her breath. Shoppers and coffee shop patrons turned to watch, and she quickly picked up the pile of bits and pieces scattered under the table. Horrified at their spectacle—two grandmothers crawling around on the floor—odds and ends were unceremoniously collected and hastily stowed. Then, standing and dusting herself off, she turned to Carol and said, "That's it. Let's go."

As they left, a distinguished middle-aged man in a tweed jacket nodded and smiled. Joyce felt uncomfortable. But when he took a seat at their vacated table, she felt relieved to discover it was a thank-you rather than a chuckle at her expense.

"Let's find a book store," she said, hoping to put the humiliating experience behind her.

"Good idea," agreed her companion, "This street appears to have everything. And, don't you love the bells and ivy draped around the lamp posts."

The time passed quickly, and Joyce found them once again boarding the Lone Star coach. Thankfully, Carol agreed to spend the time browsing through books, and they hadn't joined the bustle at the Christmas festival two blocks down from the antique store. She was pleasantly surprised to find her latest novel on the shelves. Then she was tickled when Carol recognized she was the author and flattered when she purchased a copy.

It was Carol's turn at the window. After tossing her purchases in the overhead, she settled into the seat. "The first thing I'm going to do is check my phone messages."

"I don't have mine on," Joyce said.

"Really? I don't think I could live without checking in. Aren't you worried you'll miss something important?"

"Never."

Joyce's tote was too heavy to lift into the overhead rack; now that she'd added the children's books. She shoved it under the seat. "Extended car warranties, senior benefits, the Sheriff's department. I get nothing but solicitations. Or scam risks. Not true calls from real people. The kids were in Cozumel, dining with a princess or a rodent, even if they wanted to call me."

"What about Facebook? Don't you want to check your account? What about your fans?"

"Carol, you are too sweet. I'm not Elizabeth Gilbert or Lorna Barrett with hundreds or millions of followers. So, no, I don't usually go online. I do the minimum I can get away with and only post once in a while. There is nothing social from me on my social media."

Carol wrinkled her nose. "Okay. I think I'll take a peek at mine, anyway."

"And, I think I'll nap before the evening and the late dinner show."

Finally, at Graceland, Joyce discovered the overheated bus hadn't prepared her for the weather. She stepped off the bus, zipped her coat, and tied the woolen scarf around her neck. It had to be in the forties, if not the thirties. With the sun down, Tennessee was nothing like Texas, dipping into temperatures likely to chill her through. Their luggage was whisked off, and they were hustled to the plaza for the walking Christmas tour. Thankfully, she'd foreseen the need and pulled a lined jacket from her tote.

Carol shivered in only her snowman sweater. The tour guide greeted them while handing out oversized green parkas with *Christmas with The King* printed on the back. Joyce was sure Elvis wasn't the appropriate king; however, her seatmate had no qualms and snatched one up. Swallowed in a garment three times too large, Carol appeared happy. Although, without it, her zest might have kept her warm.

Graceland Christmas Tours led them over the mansion grounds decorated for the holidays. Greens, reds, whites, everywhere lights sparkled. A young guide's running commentary included stories of what it was like to spend Christmas at Graceland, and he pointed out the beautiful exhibits and festive lawn décor, which he explained was part of Elvis' annual decorating tradition. Afterward, they were invited to visit Elvis Presley's Memphis Entertainment Complex, Presley Motors Automobile Museum, Elvis Entertainer Career Museum, and the Elvis Discovery Exhibits. But, unfortunately, Joyce had already had *"just a hunk-a-hunk"* too much of Elvis and opted for dinner. "What time do we eat?" she asked.

Carol snuggled into her oversized coat and said, "I'm ready, but first, let me see if I can buy this parka."

Dinner was a success. Not only did they see an Elvis, a whole chorus line of impersonators dressed in sequin-laden jumpsuits performed. There was enough hip wiggling to send Carol to heaven. Joyce didn't feel like she could take another gyration when they finally headed to their rooms. "If your family is traveling," Carol warned, "you better check your phone before you turn in."

"Whatever for?"

"They are in a foreign country. The ship may have gone down, or one of the children might be ill. You never know."

"It unlikely April would try to contact me whatever the situation."

However, once in her room, Joyce fished the cellphone from the bottom of her Star tote. When she pushed the button, it pinged to life: seven messages—every one from April. Unfortunately, before she could listen to the first, the phone died.

Oh, great. Joyce dropped the phone onto the bed, then rooted in her suitcase until she found a power cord. *Of course, it can't be anything significant.* But before climbing under the blankets, she plugged the phone in to charge.

The alarm went off bright and early the next morning. Joyce checked the cellphone, found it fully charged, and listened to the first message.

April's voice came in loud and clear.

—Is this a scam? Why am I getting a Facebook PM from a guy I don't know? Call me—

What was a PM? Joyce skipped to the following message.

—Don't you answer your phone? I received another note. This guy claims to have your credit cards. Is this a scam or some con game? Call me back—

Credit cards? She didn't understand what April was saying, but she had her credit cards. She'd just used one yesterday at the antique store. She listened to the next.

—Now he sent a phone number and begged me to call ASAP. I don't want to get caught in a scheme that takes my money. I need to talk to you! Where are you?—

Joyce called her daughter-in-law. The phone rang eight times before April's sleepy voice answered. "H...h...hello? Mom?"

"This is Joyce, April. What's going on? Is everyone okay?"

"Yes, of course. Only, I've been getting the strangest messages on Facebook. Some guy claims he has your credit cards."

"Well, that's crazy! I have them with me here."

"He says he knows you're traveling and will need them."

"How can he... Well, that is ridiculous!" She glanced at the Star tote. "They are right in my wallet, where they should be."

"He is insistent. Have you checked your Facebook page?"

Joyce didn't answer.

"I hate to ask, but will you check for your wallet?"

Joyce gave a deep sigh. "I don't see the point, but yes. Hold on. I'll put you on speaker." She laid the phone on the nightstand and picked up the heavy tote, groping for the wallet without success. Then she unloaded the top items: two books, a copy of the itinerary, napkins, Kleenex, an address book, a head scarf, a rain hat, and a bag of trail mix.

"Do you have them?"

"Just a minute, April. It's a big bag. Everything finds its way to the bottom."

"Dump it out on the bed."

Joyce felt panicked. Where was her wallet? "Okay. Dumping."

The contents spilled over the covers—clothing, headwraps, papers, pencils, do-dads, and whatnot. No wallet. Her stomach fell. "My wallet isn't where I thought. Give me a minute to look through my other things."

There was silence on April's side of the conversation. Joyce wondered what she was thinking. She had no desire to let her daughter-in-law take control. "I'm going to check through my things and call you back. All right?"

"Yes. But Joyce, I don't want you caught in the middle of a scam targeting seniors. So call me back one way or the other."

"I'm sure I have them," she said, but she wasn't sure.

A search of the room didn't turn them up. Joyce went downstairs and found Carol in the restaurant with a heaping plate from the breakfast buffet. Joyce scooted into the seat across from her. "Good morning. Do you know how to get onto the bus?"

Her companion dabbed her lips with a napkin and said, "You would need to find the bus driver, I suppose. What's up?"

"I took your advice about the phone and discovered my wallet is missing. I hope it is on the bus." Joyce eyed Carol's breakfast. "I could do with a coffee too. Only I'm a little worried right now."

"Look, there is our tour director." Joyce turned to find their leader talking to the couple sitting two booths down. "Ask her when you can get on the bus. I don't think we leave for an hour or two."

After a quick conversation, Joyce returned to Carol. "I can get on the bus now, look around, and be back in time for a bite. Hold down the fort. I'll join you in two shakes."

Thirty minutes later, Joyce had searched around their bus seats, in the overhead, and every inch of the coach floor. Her wallet wasn't there. She returned to the room and went through everything again. *Nada.* Her heart fell.

Returning to the buffet, she sat down heavily across from her friend. "I have lost my wallet."

Carol's eyes widened.

"And what's more, someone has it, and they contacted my daughter-in-law."

"Ransome?"

"I don't know." She wanted to cry. "Do you know how to get messages on Facebook?"

"Yes. But I don't see how—"

"He contacted her through Facebook Messenger. Maybe he contacted me, too."

"Do you have your phone?"

Joyce nodded.

She felt foolish, but after fumbling with the tiny keys, and with Carol's help, she opened a message from Alex Monroe. He had her wallet and all its contents which he'd found at the antique shop in Little Rock. Please call. He included a Houston area phone number.

Joyce ordered a second cup of stout coffee. When it arrived, she said, "I'm going to go to my room where it is quieter. There, I'm going to call this man."

"Is that wise?"

"I'll be careful. I won't give him anything he doesn't already have. I won't agree to buy any gift cards. He is from home unless he has figured out a way to spoof the system."

"Do you want me to come?"

"No. Enjoy your breakfast. I'll be back shortly." She hoped that was the case.

Once in the room, she plugged the power cord into the phone to have enough juice for a long conversation. Why had this happened during the Christmas holidays when she should have been filled with Christmas spirit? Instead, she couldn't muster a spark of joy.

She punched in the number to call Alex Monroe.

When he answered, she put as much confidence into her voice as she could summon.

"Hello? This is Joyce Hanschu."

"Thank goodness. I've been worried about you." He had a kind voice, not blustery and not pushy. However, she didn't want to be taken in and answered firmly.

"Well, you can stop. I'm here, and I am fine."

"You have no idea how much trouble it has been to find you."

Soft music played in the background on his end of the call. Joyce thought she recognized the carol *Do You Hear What I Hear?*

"First, I want to say I know what it's like to be compromised while you're traveling."

"How do you know I'm traveling?"

He gave a polite chuckle. "I found your wallet in Little Rock. Your driver's license was issued in Texas. Your home address is in

Houston. Therefore, you are not home unless someone else is traveling with all your identification."

"What do you want?"

"I want to return your items."

"What is the catch?"

There was silence on his end. The music changed to *Oh, Christmas Tree*. It was one of her favorites, reminding her of last year's family gathering, the roaring fire, opening gifts, and being surrounded by her loved ones. She felt alone.

He interrupted her thoughts. "I took the table in the coffee shop when you and your friend departed," he said. "You were well away when I left and stumbled over a package, which turned out to be your wallet."

"I tried to spot you at the festival. I didn't. I walked up one side of the street and then the other. It was useless. You were away from home, and so was I. The blue Lone Star bag told me you were either on a bus tour or had been on one."

"I am on a Christmas tour now." She caught her breath. Maybe she shouldn't have told him that; he had her home address.

"I was afraid you'd say that. Inside your wallet, I learned a lot about you. Unfortunately, it didn't contain a mobile phone number. I know where you live, how old you are, and that you're willing to donate your organs. And, more importantly, that you have an unusual surname, Hanschu."

"It's not that odd."

"Maybe not, but luckily, when I went on Facebook, I only found eight Hanschu profiles. I found your author page right away. Nice credentials, by the way. Unfortunately, when I left a message, I got no response."

"Thank you. Well, I don't check social media every day."

"I sent private messages to all eight. People are suspicious of unsolicited messages. Especially from people they don't know. I hoped at least one would be a relative and pass it on."

"Did you leave a PM for my daughter-in-law?"

"Maybe," he said apologetically. "I wanted to return your wallet before you left the area."

"I'm afraid I'm already gone."

"I don't want to mail your wallet to you. You'll need it before you get home. Maybe we can meet?"

Joyce thought for a moment. Alex Monroe sounded sincere. It was the season of hope and good cheer. Why not? "I'm at Graceland. The bus leaves in about an hour for Birmingham. I can't meet you anywhere, my schedule isn't my own, and we're attending the Nutcracker tonight and then on to Atlanta in the morning."

"Perfect! Ballet doesn't come more Christmassy than Birmingham Royal Ballet's Nutcracker. I can find you before the performance?"

"You'd travel all the way to Alabama to return my wallet?"

"Like the wise men following the star. Mine will just be on wheels."

It was a perfect gift—kindness from a stranger. The nutcracker performance would be well attended, and if Alex Monroe didn't look trustworthy, she'd still feel perfectly safe in the crowd. "How will you find me?"

"First, I'll watch for a big blue coach. Then I'll find a stunning gray-headed author waiting at the box office window. Dress for the season and bring your friend. I'll be in a tweed jacket with a sprig of holly in the lapel."

Joyce couldn't wait to tell Carol. But first, she needed to do a kindness of her own, namely, calling April to confess.

Loud music almost drowned April's voice when she answered. Finally, childish giggles and mandolins finished the job. "April? April, are you there?"

More noise, and then all went quiet. "Joyce? Sorry, the morning parade was underway, and the children didn't want to miss it. Everything okay?"

"Yes. You were right to worry. Unfortunately, I misplaced my credit cards, which was not a hoax or a scam. A very nice gentleman found them, and I have the situation under control."

"That's a relief. You can tell me all about it, but first, tell me when you get into Atlanta?"

"Tomorrow night. We have a Christmas tour, and I start the bus trip back to Houston on Friday."

"Jeff and I have been talking. We were worried about you, and the truth is it doesn't feel like Christmas without you. The kids miss you. And, we hoped...I hoped...Anyway, can you leave the tour on Friday? Our cruise will be over, and instead of taking the return bus, we'd like to meet you in Atlanta. Jeff can book rooms at the Four Seasons for all of us. We can be together and celebrate a real family Christmas. Just the Hanschu family—the whole family."

Joyce wasn't convinced it was April's idea, but her heart fluttered all the same. Maybe she had misjudged her daughter-in-law. Or perhaps, Jeff had finally put his foot down?

She couldn't wait to share the news with her new friend, Carol.

It was going to be a joyous Christmas after all.

Charlie the Menace

By:
DC Gomez

Author D.C. Gomez

D.C. Gomez is an award-winning USA Today Bestselling Author, Podcaster, motivational speaker, and coach. Born in the Dominican Republic, she grew up in Salem, Massachusetts. D.C. studied film and television at New York University. After college, she joined the US Army, and proudly served for four years.

D.C. has a master's degree in Science Administration from the Central Michigan University, as well as a Master in Adult Education from Texas A&M- Texarkana University. She is a certified John Maxwell Team speaker and coach, and a certified meditation instructor from the Chopra Center.

One of D.C. passions is helping those around her overcome their self-limiting beliefs. She writes both non-fiction as well as fiction books, ranging from Urban Fantasy to Children's Books. To learn more about her books and her passion, you can find her at www.dcgomez-author.com.

Charlie the Menace
〜

Part 1

Saint Peter was having a glorious morning. The number of souls that reported to the gates for in-processing into heaven were less than fifty. No major delays had occurred, that included the appearances of confused souls who weren't sure if they were dead or runaway Santas. Saint Peter stretched his arms over his head, taking in the radiance of the gates.

"This is exactly how Christmas Eve should be," Saint Peter said to the gates. "Peaceful, beautiful, and all in order."

The gates never replied, but Saint Peter was sure they understood him. He grabbed a rag and window spray from his magical podium. He could find anything and everything imaginable inside that podium. It was better than Mary Poppins' bag in Peter's opinion. Whistling to himself, Peter strolled to the gates for one last polishing before he closed the gates for Christmas. The gates to heaven were immaculate, but Peter enjoyed the ritual. It made him feel productive and efficient.

Pssst

Peter stopped as the strange sound reached him. He looked

over his shoulder, but nobody was around. Giving the area one last look, he shook his head and went back to polishing.

Pssst. Peter.

There it is again, Peter thought. *I didn't imagine it.*

Peter turned around and marched over to his podium. Dropping the rag and window spray back inside the cabinet, Peter examined his surroundings. Nothing seemed out of place. Except...

Since when is there a giant boulder next to the trail? Peter asked himself.

He was ready to inspect when the boulder moved forward. Peter jumped. He grabbed his tablet from the top of the podium – Heaven edition, because technology is faster and more reliable in heaven, of course. Without a second thought, Peter activated the emergency system. Whatever was roaming the grounds could not enter heaven. With a soft chime, the gates locked, and the entrance was secure.

Peter gave the gates one last look and nodded to himself. He slowly reached inside the podium and pulled out a large golden scythe. If demons were planning to breach his terrain, Peter had other plans for them. He tip-toed toward the boulder. His movements were not as smooth as he wished because of his tailored suit. His outfit was impeccable, but not meant for battle.

This outfit was not meant for clandestine operations, Peter told himself. *I will request a new design after Christmas. My movements can't be restricted when I'm on duty.*

Less than ten feet away from the boulder, Peter adjusted his scythe over his head, ready to strike. He charged the last few feet with a loud cry.

"Freeze!" shouted Peter.

"Aghhh! What in God's name are you doing? Are you trying to kill me?" Saint James replied.

"Me?" Peter shouted back. "You're the one sneaking around. What were you thinking? And why are you hiding behind that boulder?"

"I wasn't sneaking into the gates," James told him. "I was trying to get your attention."

"Why?" Peter asked, inspecting his friend. "What are you wearing?"

While Peter had a black designer suit on, James was casually dressed in jeans and a t-shirt. His t-shirt, unfortunately, was untucked and had stains on the front.

"You realize jeans went out of fashion in heaven in the '90s," Peter said. "Please tell me you don't have the jean jacket to go with that assemble?"

"I was not wearing this around heaven," James clarified.

"Where else were you wearing that monstrosity?" Peter asked.

"That's not important," James tried to stop the conversation.

"Of course, it's important," Peter corrected. "We have standards to maintain here. If we don't do it, who will?"

"Can we please focus?" James asked, as the veins on the side of his head bulged. "I have a slight problem and need your help."

"More problems than your fashion sense?" Peter leaned on his scythe, inspecting James again.

James reached behind the boulder and pulled a small child with curly brown hair and big brown eyes next to him. The child was busy playing with James' phone.

"Oh God!" Peter jumped to attention. "Is that yours? No wait. That's impossible. Where did you find him?"

Peter leaned down and glanced at the child. James took his phone away from the child. The boy reached for the phone but failed. Instead, he concentrated on freeing himself from James' hold on his shoulder. James held on tighter and glared down at the kid.

"Obviously, not mine," James answered, still looking at the child.

"So . . . why is he here?" Peter bent down to examine the boy. "James, have you lost your mind?"

"I haven't lost my mind, but this little one is lost," James admitted.

"Okay," Peter said, standing back to his full height. "That doesn't explain why he's in heaven."

James took a deep breath and rubbed his short black hair, avoiding Peter's eyes.

"He was praying," James confessed.

"I don't get it," Peter replied.

"Peter." James took another deep breath before jumping in. "He is five years old and prayed with a faith so strong his words reached my ears here in heaven. When was the last time somebody prayed with such intensity to draw our attention?"

Peter was silent for a minute. The small boy played with a patch of clouds that flew in his direction. He giggled with joy at the fluffy things moving around him.

"What are you planning to do with him?" Peter asked softly. "I'm sure someone is looking for him."

"I'm going to go search for his parents," James announced, smiling at his friend.

"That's a reasonable plan," Peter told him. "But why do you need my help?"

"I need you to watch him. I can't walk around earth with a small child," James explained. "I'll look suspicious."

"What?" Peter snapped his head in James' direction. "What are you talking about?"

"With all the weirdoes and madness going on down there, walking around asking strangers if this kid belongs to them just sounds wrong," James stated. "What if the wrong person claims him?"

"We can't have a living child in heaven," Peter whined.

"He is not in heaven," James corrected him. "He is at the gates, so it's not the same. As long as he doesn't go in it's all good."

"I don't know." Peter tapped his fingers on the scythe.

"I'll volunteer to take the cleaning course with the Cherubs," added James.

"You can't wiggle your way out of it at the last minute," Peter demanded. "I'm not going in if I have to do your dirty work here."

"I'll be there bright an early New Year's Day," James raised his free hand in salute.

"Deal," said Peter. "Anything I need to know about this kid?"

"Nothing major," James said, looking up as he searched his memories. "He is hyper, but so is every five-year-old. You should be fine. Nothing to worry about."

"You sound suspicious," said Peter. "I'm supposed to be closing up everything before sunset. So, hurry."

"I'll be back as soon as I find one of his parents," James replied, handing the small boy over. "Good luck Peter,"

Before Peter could ask what he meant, James was gone. Peter knelt down, using his scythe for balance, and smiled at the little boy.

"What's your name, dear?" Peter asked.

"Charlie," replied the boy, staring at Peter's scythe. "What's that?"

Peter followed Charlie's gaze and smiled. "It's a scythe."

"What is it for?" Charlie asked.

"Protection."

"Protection from what?" Charlie continued his interrogation.

"From anything trying to break in," Peter struggled to find the right things to say.

"Do you have a lot of things breaking in?" Charlie was not slowing down.

"We do not."

"So why do you have it?" pushed Charlie.

"Because it's better to be safe," Peter answered, standing up. "And it's time I returned to the gates. Come with me."

Peter extended his hand, but Charlie hesitated.

"It's okay, Charlie," Peter said in a soft voice. "We're just going to move closer to the gates so I can get things ready. You're safe, I promise."

Charlie glanced around the open space, the road made of gold bricks, and the golden gate in front of him. With a smile, he took Peter's hand and walked toward the gate.

"Am I going in?" Charlie asked softly, still transfixed by the luminous light.

"Not yet, dear," Peter answered. "You still have lots of living to do."

As they arrived at the gates, Peter realized there was no place for Charlie to sit. They walked toward the podium, and Peter opened the door. Reaching inside, he pulled out a patio chair with bright red cushions.

"Wow," exclaimed Charlie. "What else do you have in there?"

Peter grabbed Charlie's shoulder before he jumped inside the podium.

"You do not want to go in there," Peter told him.

"Why not?"

"Because we would never find you again," Peter admitted. "How about you sit in this comfy chair while I do my inspections?"

"What am I doing?"

"Sitting," Peter replied.

"And what else?" Charlie continued.

"Just sitting," Peter explained.

"But that's boring," said Charlie, pouting.

"Well . . ." Peter looked around his podium for inspiration.

Trying to buy himself some time, Peter took a few steps away from his podium to arrange the chair with its cushions.

"Charlie, how about you have a sit here and I'll get you . . ." Peter trailed off, searching his brain. "I'm going to find you something. Just wait there."

Peter rushed to the podium. *What do I have in here for a kid?* Almost as if the podium had read Peter's mind, it provided a stack of books and crayons.

"I love you," Peter said to his podium, rubbing the horizontal surface. "Okay, Charlie, I have some books and coloring supplies. This should be fun."

As Peter walked toward Charlie, he read the titles provided by the podium. The first book was a picture book called "*Charlie, What's your talent?*"

"Look, I even found one with your name," Peter told Charlie, full of excitement. "Isn't this great?"

"Does it really have my name?" Charlie asked, giving Peter a side glare.

"Yes, it does." Peter showed the child the cover of the book. "Now, while you sit there and read these, I'm going to secure the gates."

"Okay," said Charlie, as Peter covered the rest of the chair in books and crayons.

Why was James worried? This is a no brainer. Peter smiled to himself and worked on his inventory of souls for the day.

THUMP!

The sound came from behind Peter, and he quickly spun around. To his horror, Charlie was gone, and all the books were dumped on the ground.

"Oh God," Peter said to the empty chair as he rushed toward it. "I need to have a word with that author. That girl needs longer children's books. Charlie, where are . . ."

Peter didn't finish the statement as the gate's alarms blared to life. Peter turned around so quickly that he tripped over his own feet. Landing on his behind, he stared at the gates, trying to make sense of what his eyes were seeing. Charlie was climbing the gates at a fairly rapid speed for a five-year-old.

"Step away from the gates," the friendly gate security system announced. "This is your last warning. We will take drastic measures to eliminate the intruder."

"I really need to work on that message," Peter said to the gates as he struggled to get to his feet. "Charlie, get down from there."

Charlie was not paying any attention to Peter's demands. Instead, he dangled from the gate and tapped all the shining lights reflecting from its surface.

"Initiating security precautions," the gates announced in a chipper and clear voice.

"No!" shouted Peter.

Peter sprinted to his tablet and, moving his fingers over the control panels faster than most modern gamers, he disengaged the electric shock waves.

"Alarms off," the gates announced.

Peter took long breaths, willing his heart to slow down.

"Peter, is everything alright?" a voice asked from the intercom system on the podium. "We're getting ready to deploy the security guards."

"No need for that," shouted Peter. "Everything is fine."

"Are you sure?" the voice asked.

"Yes," Peter replied. "Just one of James' pranks activated the gates."

Peter wasn't technically lying. He just didn't need a squad of killer Cherubs charging the gates and turning Charlie into toast.

"Please inform James, this is not funny," the voice demanded, disconnecting the call.

"Oh, trust me," said Peter. "James and I will have plenty of words."

With the gates' security system in standby mode, Peter marched over. Charlie was halfway up the gates when Peter reached him.

"Charlie, get down from there," Peter said in a stern voice with his hands on his hips.

Peter inhaled deeply, but the veins on his forehead were pulsating. He rubbed his hands on his pants, even though he knew there was no way he was sweating.

How on earth am I going to explain this kid climbing the gates? Peter asked himself.

"But I see birdies up there," Charlie said.

"I'm sure they're beautiful, but the gates are not for climbing," Peter added.

Charlie was not interested in Peter's reply. Instead, he kept on climbing. Left with little alternatives, Peter returned to the podium. Searching inside, he found a small lift and took it out. Peter was planning to have a long discussion with James once he returned. Back at the gates, Peter climbed the lift, pressed a few buttons, and quickly reached Charlie's level.

"Charlie, time to get off," Peter told the child.

Charlie ignored him and climbed a little higher. Wasting no more time, Peter took hold of Charlie by the waist and pulled. To Peter's surprise, Charlie was holding on to the gates like a watermelon vine hooks to a fence. Charlie was not coming off as easily as Peter expected.

"Charlie, I really need you to get down," Peter said, grinding his teeth.

"It's boring down there," said Charlie.

"What if I give you a balloon?" Peter asked, hoping to God his podium had a balloon somewhere.

"Really?" Charlie looked over his shoulder.

"Yes," Peter answered.

"Yes!" Charlie let go of the gates without another warning, making Peter fumble to keep his hold on the child.

"How have you survived this long in the world?" Peter asked, placing Charlie slowly next to him.

"Balloon!" Charlie replied.

Prayers. I need more prayers. Peter told himself.

Engaging the lift, Peter brought them both down to the ground. If he survived this child, James was going to pay for this.

"Balloon," Charlie repeated, jumping off the lift.

Peter followed at a slower pace, taking deep breaths and adjusting his tie. Charlie took Peter's hand and dragged him down toward the podium.

Please, have a balloon. Peter prayed to his podium.

As they neared the magical device, Charlie was bouncing up and down with joy. Peter held his breath and slowly opened the podium's compartment door. With a soft breeze, dozens of colorful balloons floated out of the thing. Peter's mouth dropped open, as Charlie ran in circles chasing the floating balls.

"Oh, thank you, thank you." Peter hugged his podium in gratitude as Charlie ran around chasing his new toys. "Let's try to get everything secure before he does anything else crazy."

Peter faced his tablet and started his end of the day closing procedures but couldn't focus. Every thirty seconds, he looked up to search for Charlie. He didn't want to lose sight of the child. But after several long, painful minutes of going back and forth between Charlie and his tablet, Peter gave up. This was not working out for him. Rubbing his temples, he looked for Charlie.

"Oh God." Peter stopped the massaging and searched the area. "Where did you go?"

The landscaping of heaven was, as usual, picture perfect and serene. That was the problem, too serene and no Charlie. Close to his location toward the right of the gates, he saw a flash of lightning, followed by a child's high pitch cry of "Whoopee."

"Why me?" cried Peter as he rushed in the direction of the clouds.

Peter couldn't believe it. Charlie was bouncing from cloud to cloud, doing somersaults. "What are you doing?"

"I'm making it rain," Charlie replied.

"That's not how we make rain here," Peter told the child, but stopped as he glanced over the edge of the cloud.

The blessing, or in the case for Peter, his curse, was being able to know every location on earth from his post on the gates. This made for quick rescue missions when a soul ran away back to earth. Unfortunately, for Peter the sight he witnessed as he stared down to earth was not a typical one for Christmas Eve.

A massive downpour was hitting the earth at rapid speed. Peter held his breath. "Flooding in Kansas was not on the forecast for this evening."

Taking his gaze away from the downpour, Peter climbed the soggy cloud. Charlie was enjoying his very own Olympic size trampoline.

"Okay, Charlie, we need to get off now," said Peter, reaching for the child.

Charlie leapt in the air and landed on several clouds opposite Peter. The sound of rolling rocks filled the air. Peter swallowed hard and peaked down over the clouds.

"Hail in Texas is going to cause some tension today." Peter closed his eyes. "Charlie, we really need to go."

"But I'm having fun," Charlie said.

"I know," Peter told him, as the clouds bounced him around. "How about food?"

"I want chicken nuggets!" Charlie screamed.

Before Peter could reply, Charlie was running down the clouds toward the podium. Peter slumped his shoulders and climbed out of the clouds, his feet and suit wet. Charlie turned around and rushed back to Peter.

"Let's go." Charlie grabbed Peter's hand and dragged him across the field.

Peter shook his head. *How am I going to explain the weather to the big guy?*

"Hurry up," Charlie demanded.

"I'm coming," said Peter. "Let me grab a table before we start."

Peter stopped in front of the podium and reached inside the door. It didn't take him long to pull out a small table. Grabbing Charlie's hand, just in case the small demon ran away again, he walked toward the chair. He placed Charlie in the chair and arranged the table in front of him.

"Okay Charlie, what would you like to eat?" asked Peter, pulling his cell phone from his pocket.

"Chicken nuggets, ice cream, fries, a hot-fudge shake, apple pie, slushy, and lots of ketchup," Charlie finished, placing his order with a smile. "And Pizza."

"Are you going to eat all that?" Peter asked, glancing between Charlie and his app for the food items in heaven.

"I'm a growing boy," Charlie replied.

"With a tape-worm," said Peter under his breath. "Let me complete this and we should be all set."

With one last click on the app, Peter finished placing the order. As he placed his phone back in his pocket, the table in front of Charlie glowed.

"Ohhhh, look!" Charlie shouted.

As Charlie clapped in excitement, all his food appeared on the table.

"It's like Harry Potter," Charlie announced.

"Right, minus the enslaved house-elves," Peter replied, confusing the small boy, who glanced back at him with a frown on his face. "Never mind. But aren't you a little too young to be reading that?"

"My daddy let me watch all the movies," Charlie answered, stuffing a French fry in his mouth.

Peter shook his head. "Of course."Peter shook his head.

Charlie was inhaling his food with an enormous grin on his face. At that moment, Peter smiled. Charlie was truly a young child full of happiness and joy. He even ate with the joy that only the young and innocent have.

"Tell me, Charlie," Peter asked softly. "What made you pray today?"

"My mommy," Charlie answered in between bites.

"What about your mommy?"

"She said, anytime I feel afraid, to pray," Charlie said, looking up at Peter. "Mommy says God will never leave me alone, and I should not be afraid."

"Your mommy is a smart lady," Peter told him. "Chew your food."

"Okay," Charlie replied, but didn't bother chewing for too long.

Peter walked back to his podium and pulled out a chair for himself. At least Charlie was still, for now. Peter was not used to running around heaven, or anywhere else for that matter. He was a saint for God's sake. No respectable saint does this much physical activity. He dropped his head in his hands and closed his eyes. Making all these reports was going to take forever. At least he didn't sweat in heaven. That would be like adding insult to injury.

"Mr. Peter, I'm done," Charlie shouted from his seat.

"You are?" Peter asked, opening his eyes. "How?"

Charlie climbed down from his chair and ran toward Peter. "Let's play tag"

"No wait," said Peter, reaching for the child. "You got ketchup on your shirt, and red stains on your cheeks. How did you get crumbs in your hair? We need to get you clean."

"Tag!" Peter didn't have time to finish his list of things to clean when the child punched him in the leg. Before Peter could react, Charlie was running down the gold brick road like a bat out of hell.

"Oh Lord, save me," said Peter to the gates, struggling to get to his feet.

As he took one long deep breath, the immaculate and always respectable saint took off running down the road.

Saints are not supposed to run. Peter reminded himself.

Part 2

Peter lost track of time. Had it been four or was it five hours since lunch time? He didn't know and at the moment he didn't care. All he wanted to do was sleep. His feet hurt, which was almost impossible since he wore the heaven edition of the Milani. The Italian Loafers were better than walking on clouds. To make things more ridiculous in Peter's mind, he was walking on clouds, yet his feet ached. His tie was missing, and his perfectly starched white shirt was stained.

Peter glanced at his body from his sprawled position on the ground, and the sight was a disaster. He couldn't move. The last round of paintball got him. For a five-year-old, Charlie had an extremely accurate aim. Peter's groin, biceps, and even his right cheek ached. Thank God for his safety glasses or he would have lost an eye.

Could saints go blind? Peter asked himself as he dropped his head back down to the clouds. *At least Charlie was finally sleeping.*

"What in God's name happened here?" James' voice woke Peter from his momentary daze.

"Shhhh," hissed Peter, struggling to stand. "Can't you see Charlie is asleep?"

"I see that, and you as well," James corrected.

"There is no sleep with this little monster," Peter whispered. "Where have you been? I almost died these last five hours."

"What are you talking about?" James asked, folding his arms over his chest. "I was gone less than two."

"Has it only been two hours?" Peter rubbed his face, staring blankly at the sky. "I barely survived."

"You survived." James was struggling not to yell. "What happened to the gates and the rest of the area? There are red, blue, and yellow stains on the gates."

"That's just paint."

"There is whipped cream on the gold road," James continued.

"We can power-wash that," Peter added, waving his hands around.

"And the chocolate syrup dripping from the trees and the clouds?" James pointed at the disaster zone down the road.

"They needed some excitement in their day." Peter dropped to the ground as James glared.

"Do you know there are hundreds of angel sightings on clouds all over earth?" The question was not a happy one, as James tapped his foot in front of Peter.

"I'm sure we have converted tons of new believers." Peter yawned and dropped his head back. "It's not my fault you left me with a child that has more stamina than the energizer bunny on crack. There is no off button with him."

"Peter, this is serious," James announced.

"He is alive and fed."

"You fed him?" James asked, looking over Charlie, who was curled on his side asleep on a bed of clouds and pillows. "Please tell me no sugar."

"Of course, I didn't give him sugar," Peter said, shaking his head. "That stuff tastes nasty. I gave him the things all kids love to eat — nuggets, fries, shakes, ice cream, slushy — what else?"

"Peter, that's all sugar," James forced himself to keep his voice under control.

"Fries are not sugar, or the chicken," Peter corrected him, as he opened one eye.

"Fine, maybe not those," James admitted. "But everything else is. It's like adding gasoline to a fire. You just fueled him."

"Well, that explains a lot," Peter sighed. "This is all your fault."

"How is that my fault?"

"Next time you bring Charlie the Menace to heaven, bring user instructions with him," Peter chastised his friend. "When was the last time I babysat a human kid? Millennia ago. How was I supposed to know this?"

"You have television with all the prime channels How don't you know this?" James reprimanded him.

"Don't get sassy with me," Peter told his friend. "You owe me big time."

James took a deep breath and stretched his arms over his head. He glanced around the space and saw cake covering the boulder he used earlier.

"Do you have a status update, or did you just stop by to disturb my sleep?" Peter disrupted James' musings.

"I found his mother," James told Peter. "She has been frantic looking for him. I think it's time to take him home."

"That's a great idea," Peter agreed, making himself get to a sitting position. "Try not to wake him."

"I doubt he would wake even for an earthquake," James told

him. "He probably crashed from all the junk food and whatever extreme game you two were playing."

"His mom is very lucky," Peter said to James. "He is truly a sweet kid. Overwhelming. But sweet."

"I have a feeling she has a new appreciation for him," James informed him. "I'm going to deliver this little one. When I get back, I'll help you clean up."

"No rush at all," said Peter, dropping his head back on the ground made of fluffy clouds. "I'll be right here taking a nap."

Peter was out by the time James picked up Charlie. Paint stains were all over Charlie's clothes. His curly brown hair was matted, and he smelled of sugar and cotton candy.

"Hi Mr. James," said Charlie, opening one little eye. "Are we going home?"

"Yes, we are," James answered. "Your mom is very worried about you."

"I miss mommy," Charlie told him, dropping his head over James' shoulder.

"I'm glad you do," James told him. "But let's clean you up a little. We don't need your family panicking about your current condition."

With a snap of his finger, the young boy was spotless. Charlie's hair was back in a combed clean condition, and he smelled of jasmine.

"Much better," James told Charlie. "Don't go anywhere Peter, I'll be back."

"Uh huh," Peter rambled.

James shook his head and smiled. Saint Peter, the Rock of heaven, defeated by five-year-old, Charlie the Menace. James dragged his phone from his pocket without disturbing Charlie. He took several photos of poor Saint Peter's disheveled state, and a special selfie with Charlie and Peter in the background.

"I know exactly what Peter is getting for the Three Wisemen Day," James said to the sleeping Charlie. "At least I didn't tie-dye the gates last time I was in charge."

Leaving Saint Peter to dose off in the beautiful afternoon, James made his way back to earth. He glanced at Charlie and smirked.

"The magic of children," James said out loud, and disappeared with a little pop to deliver the child back to his mother.

The End... For now!

A Long
Winter's Nap
By:
Sherry Hall

Author Sherry Hall

Sherry Hall is an author and educator in Texas. She loves travel, art and Christmas. Her work has appeared in Chicken Soup for the Soul The Wonder of Christmas, First Magazine for Women and Fueled by Coffee and Love the Refill, stories for teachers. She is the author of several books including The Charming Bracelet, The Charming Christmas Bracelet, LuAnne's Knit and Pearl, Whomp, Vert, Arthur Bean's Map of the World and The Mermaid's Locket. She is co-author of the Crossrut Motocross Series. You can find her online at:

www.sherryhallwrites.com

Or

https://sherryville.livejournal.com

A Long Winter's Nap

C amille Forester turned the key in the front door lock and shoved the door hard with her hip. It groaned as it opened. The sound gave her a quick stab of pain. If Hank were alive he would have never let the hinges rust like that. She staggered toward the kitchen weighed down with grocery sacks and assorted gift bags and boxes. As she slowly made her way to the table to deposit her many parcels and packages, she had to carefully weave around the world's three yappiest dogs.

"Okay, okay! Gimme just a second!" she begged the mutts.

Millie plopped everything down on the old table with a resounding thud, opened the back door for Chester, Barney, and Rat and then ran for the restroom for herself. It had been a long day. The last week before school let out for the winter holidays always was a challenging time and the last day was always barely controlled chaos. The students were ramped up and hardly any learning went on, the teachers were tired, and the school building itself seemed to be begging for a break. Well they had made it. Checking out after early dismissal, Millie made several stops on the way home to get supplies for Christmas. Her own grown children, Mitch, Ella, and Daisy, would all arrive tomorrow morning with their spouses and children of their own in tow. It had been several years since they had all been in one place for the holiday and Mille was looking forward to it, even though there was much work to be done to prepare.

Back in the kitchen, she let the dogs back in and started putting away groceries as she reflected on the day. The energy and extra events had drained her. The singalong, the decorations, all of it. Her students were precious seven year olds, but after 29 years of teaching second grade, Millie found herself looking toward retirement just a couple of years away.

Retirement.

The thought plunged her into sadness just as her squeaky door hinges had. Retirement was something she and Hank were supposed to enjoy together and he had been so rude as to suddenly up and die this past summer of a heart attack. Maybe now she should just push through and keep working. Stay busy. Forget about those plans for adventure and spontaneity. Lesson planning and schedules were what she knew after all. Millie sighed. This first holiday without him was going to be so difficult and it wasn't lost on Millie that in part this was the reason her children were gathering around her this year. Well, that was a blessing she supposed.

Putting away the last of the cold groceries, she left the rest of the food on the counter and opened a bottle of ruby claret. After pouring a large glass of the fragrant red wine, she meandered to her big, plush leather couch perusing the various gifts awaiting wrap.

I will just rest for a little bit and then get to work, she thought to herself. Millie took a sip of the wine and leaned back into the leather letting it cradle her. *Hank had sure loved this couch* she remembered. He often fell asleep to the History Channel. Millie could hear his snores all the way in the bedroom. Millie took another long drink and closed her eyes.

"Millie... Millllie... CAMILLE!"

Millie jerked her eyes open and sat up fast, nearly spilling the last of the wine. Setting her glass carefully on the coffee table, she rubbed her eyes. The house was dark and still. All three pups snoozed near the hearth in front of... a blazing fire? *How in the heck...* Millie wondered. I must have really fallen asleep, but where did the fire come from? Looking around she tried to see the clock on her oven but it was dark. *Power must be out* thought Millie. She crept to the table to dig her cell out of her purse. 2:00 am!

Disoriented, Millie made her way back to the couch and began to look up the number to the power company. Before she could make the call, the last of her phone battery gave out and left Millie in the dark except the firelight.

Wrinkling her forehead, she peered again into the fire. While she was grateful for the light and warmth, she was also disturbed by it. She had not used her fireplace in months and she certainly had not set a fire before dozing off. Another nagging thought was circling her brain as well – she had heard a voice as she slept, she was almost certain. Millie shook her head to try and clear it and as she did Chester, Barney, and Rat woke up and came to the couch where they sat, expectantly looking at the empty seat next to Millie. "Now, what are you three on about?" Millie asked.

Then she heard the voice again, soft like a whispered prayer. "Millie."

Slowly, holding her breath, Millie turned to the empty couch beside her. "Hank!"

The dogs yelped. There seated next to Millie on the couch was a figure who looked for all the world like her dead husband. He laughed.

"Yes, Millie, it is me."

"But, you... how!? I... I must be dreaming," Millie sputtered, vowing to herself to never fall asleep to claret again.

"Millie," Hank said again, "you are not dreaming, but this is something similar. I...Millie, could you focus please?"

Hank fell silent and Millie managed to drag her gaze back to him from the dogs. Barney was wagging his tail, Chester had his front paws up on the couch where Hank was petting his head, and Rat seemed to be impatiently waiting his turn to say hello to Hank.

"The dogs see you too..." Millie trailed off tilting her head to the side and staring at Hank with question marks in her eyes.

"Yes, they see me. Millie, I am here with you but just for a few hours. You see, this is a very special visit from Heaven."

Millie's eyes filled with tears. "Oh Hank, I have missed you so much. I don't care if I am dreaming, or hallucinating, or whatever." Hank's gentle laugh filled the room as he reached over and took Millie's hand, warming her through and through.

"Millie, now I need to tell you some things while I am here. So, I want you to dry your tears, okay?"

Millie sniffed and used the edge of her t-shirt to swipe at the corners of her eyes as she nodded furiously. "Yes, Hank, I am listening," she replied. Hank smiled. "Okay, here we go!"

"Okay, so let me see if I got this straight," Millie was saying, "you get a one-time visit, everyone in heaven, a one-time visit back and this is yours?"

"That's about right," Hank nodded in affirmation.

"How come we never hear about this? Why now? And how long can you stay?"

"Millie, here's the thing, a lot of people never use theirs. It's Heaven after all. It's, well, it's paradise there. All the promises of the Bible, Millie, they are true. Lots of people don't want to leave. It doesn't seem like a long separation from your loved ones when you are in eternity. It is just a moment there until they are reunited with you. And then, some people save their visit just in case they feel there will be a time it is really needed. Sometimes they save it forever. Also, there are rules. It's a bit complicated. You see, I am only here until I tell you what it is you need to know."

"What I need to know?" Millie repeated puzzled.

"Yes," Hank replied, "but... well, I'm not sure you want to hear it."

"Now you have me worried," said Millie.

Hank chuckled again. "It's just, that, well, there is still so much joy for you to have here Millie. I can't be more specific – rules. But, your life isn't over yet."

"Could've fooled me." Millie sighed. Every day since Hank died had been a challenge. Many days she drove to work sobbing and then had to sit in the school parking lot for a few minutes to get the waterworks turned off before going inside. To her students and her colleagues, her church group, and even her close friends, Millie was doing okay, but inside her grief was taking on a life of its own. Some days, she was able to shove the pain way down deep inside and make it back home to the couch and the dogs before the tears came. Other days, she had to spend part of her short lunch break in the restroom trying to muffle her sobs so they wouldn't be heard in the teacher's lounge next door. Those days, she would breathe and pray as tears ran down her cheeks and dripped onto her lanyard holding her school ID. The badge had a frumpy looking picture of herself under the words Mrs. Forester. Millie looked down now to see she still had her ID around her neck. The word Mrs. seemed to jump out at her.

Millie pulled her eyes away from the badge to her husband. Hank looked just like himself, as he always had. His hair had gone gray the last year he was alive and Millie thought it looked so good on him. He wore faded blue jeans and a soft red plaid flannel shirt. Hank saw Millie looking him over and smiled. "The clothes are just so you feel comfortable, Millie. They aren't so important in Heaven."

"What are you saying? You run around naked all the time?" Millie asked.

Hank chuckled. "No, it's just, we don't exactly need our *bodies,* so we don't need the stuff for our bodies. It's kind of hard to explain. And anyway, that isn't important. Millie, I am here to tell you to go ahead and retire and find a way to enjoy your life. Life is a great gift from God, and you are wasting it just sitting on this couch crying for me and drinking too much wine every night."

Millie reddened. "Hank, I... well I just don't know who I am without you!" she cried.

"That is the problem exactly," Hank told her. "We had a beautiful life together, a good marriage, kids, everything, but don't you see Millie, you exist without me. You are still alive! Please honey, you need to embrace that gift."

"Oh Hank..." Millie looked at her husband and back into the blazing fire. "It's just... I am stuck. This grief is so big. I can't lift it."

"Stop trying to get rid of it first of all. It's okay to miss me, to be sad, but Millie, you are trying to do all of this on your own when there is a whole world of people out there to help you, not to mention the Good Lord Himself. It is time to move forward, even with your grief, and find out what your life looks like now... without me."

Hank's last words hung there in the air in front of the fire – *without me.* Millie felt she could see them take shape as clearly as reading her name badge. Frantically reaching for Hank she cried, "But you will always be with me. Right?"

This time there was no chuckle or smile. "Now Camille," Hank addressed her seriously, "I won't be with you this way ever again, but you know we will see each other in the hereafter. It just isn't time for you to turn your thoughts there yet. However, you will have another fella in your life pretty soon who is gonna take your mind off of your grief some. I think he might even go by the name Hank."

"No. Now see here, Hank, if you are going to try to convince me to date again that is not going to happen. I have no interest whatsoever –"

She was interrupted by Hank's loudest laugh yet. "Millie, that is not what I mean, but I have already said too much. And, well, I delivered the message I came to deliver. I hope you will take it to heart."

"Hank! Please don't leave! I... I don't understand."

"You will," Hank assured her. "But for now, you need to rest. Sleep. Know I am okay. Live your life and remember God is good all the time."

In a whisper Millie replied, "All the time, God is good," and she closed her eyes once again.

The whoosh of electricity returning was alarming after the deep, dark, quiet night. Millie awoke with a start, once again disoriented, and trying to hang on to the memory of Hank from her dreams. As she did most mornings, she felt his loss anew, and the pain made her catch her breath. However, this morning she had so much to do. She had to prep the meal and wrap the gifts before her family arrived in...looking at the clock Millie saw she had overslept by several hours! In a panic, she rushed to her bedroom, and peeling off yesterday's work clothes, she jumped in the shower to scrub off her day old make-up and...was that a smoky smell? The dream crept back in to her mind as she considered Hank's words. *Live your life. Retire. A new fella...*

Annoyed, Millie pushed the thoughts away. It was going to take more than a long winter's nap to fix all the demons Millie had been wrestling with since Hank passed. As Hank's wife, she had built her world around him and the kids. Even her career was chosen, because teaching allowed her to be home in the evenings and on holidays, even though there were nights she fell asleep grading papers while the family watched TV. Millie loved being married to Hank, and since he had died, she felt as if she were walking around missing a limb. Now, here he was showing up in her dreams and telling her to get on with her life without him.

Not gonna happen, Hank! Millie thought as she stared into

her closet. She reached for a pair of leggings and an oversized sweatshirt. She had just tugged them on when the doorbell rang. She ran to let the dogs out back and ran to answer the door, stopping cold as she reached for the doorknob. The presents! They were all still unwrapped on the kitchen table! Oh no. Yelling through the door that it would be just a minute, Millie spun and headed back to the kitchen table where the gifts were...gone? They were gone!

Frantically looking around, she saw them wrapped and arranged under the tree. The smell of turkey in the oven wafted toward her and the table was set and ready for the meal. Unbelieving and trying to figure out if she had cooked and wrapped in her sleep, Millie stood frozen until the doorbell rang again.

"Mom! Let us in! We are freezing out here." A chorus of voices clamored in agreement. Millie shrugged thinking *too bad I didn't light a fire too.* Then as the hearth jumped to blazing life, she ran to the door to let her family in. Mitch, Ella, and Daisy crowded in around her, red-cheeked and smiling while their spouses and kids flowed in around them until the small foyer was practically bursting with people who all seemed too talk at once.

"Mom! Gosh it smells so good!"

"You look wonderful!"

"Mimi, I made you my Christmas gift myself!"

Millie leaned into the arms of her children and exhaled. She felt a comfort she could barely describe that seemed to fill up her soul. Looking over Daisy's shoulder, she caught a glimpse of the dogs sitting quietly as Hank gave them all a pat. Then he turned toward her and with a smile, he lifted his hand and waved and faded away. Millie felt a shift in her spirit.

"Bye Hank," Millie whispered.

"Mom, what did you say?" asked Mitch.

"Hmm? Oh nothing! Let's eat I have so much to tell you all!"

Ella pushed back her plate and sighed. "Gosh Mom, everything was delicious. I don't know how you had time to prepare everything."

"I hardly know myself," said Millie. "But I am about to have some extra time on my hands." After a dramatic pause Millie announced, "I'm going to retire in June!" She couldn't believe she was hearing herself say the words, but it felt right. Hank was right. She needed to move forward in life. The people sitting around her table with her were proof that life goes on. She owed it to them, to Hank, and to herself to embrace her own life as the gift that it was. She felt a weight that she had carried since summer lift from her shoulders. She was going to retire. And she would figure out the rest later.

This news was met with claps and cheers. Ella's husband Mark replied, "Great timing!" which got him an elbow from Ella. Millie gave them a questioning look and Ella smiled. "Well Mom," she said. "I don't want to overshadow your big news, but Mark and I have an announcement too. We're pregnant!"

"Oh, Ella, honey!" Millie was overjoyed. Ella was the only one of her children who had not had kids of her own, and many a night Ella had called in tears because they couldn't seem to get pregnant. Millie knew they had visited a fertility doctor, but she rarely asked how things were going. It could be such a difficult topic for Ella. As each of the other family members embraced Ella and shook hands with Mark Ella interrupted. "There's more news." Everyone fell silent and Ella continued. "Because we have struggled with having a baby for so many years, we kept this news to ourselves for quite a while. The baby is due in April, just before you retire, Mom. We were hoping you would be able to help look after him some of the time so I can work part-time.

Millie jumped out of her chair. "Of course, I will!" she said. "That would be, wait, did you say him?"

"Yes," responded Ella. "It's a boy and, Mom, we thought, if it is okay with you, that we would like to name him after dad, Henry, but of course we will call him Hank."

Millie sat down hard in her chair.

A new fella named Hank.

Millie stared open-mouthed at her daughter.

Ella's face fell. "I mean, if you don't want us to name the baby after Dad..."

"Oh, honey, no! I mean yes I do! That would be just perfect. It just, caught me by surprise is all," Millie assured her daughter, and Ella beamed.

Daisy's husband Peter raised his glass. "A toast to good endings and to new beginnings!"

As glasses clinked and good wishes flowed, Mitch leaned over and whispered in Millie's ear, "All this moment needs is pie and it would be perfect." Millie chuckled. "Well, let's see if there is any pie," she said, as she headed into the utility room.

On holidays, pies were always laid out in the utility room because there was never enough counter space in the kitchen. Millie knew she hadn't baked any pies, but she had a pretty good idea that they would be there anyway and they were. There was pumpkin, chocolate, and buttermilk. Hank had apparently been busy during her long winter nap. Millie gathered up the pies, whispered a quick thanks to Hank, and a prayer of deep gratitude to the Lord and headed back to her family and her life.

The day unfolded in a series of sweet moments. Gifts were exchanged and enjoyed. Some of the family wandered into the backyard to throw around a football. The dishes were washed and after a few hours, people started to drift back toward the kitchen for leftovers. Millie felt a lightness in her heart that she had not felt since Hank died. She felt the blessings of her family, her home, and her new unknown future, no longer filling her with dread. Truly, God was good all the time. The back door opened and Mitch's wife Susan came in with little two-year-old Davy in tow. The boy was rubbing his eyes and whining. Susan looked at Millie. "I'm just going to go put him down in the guest room if that's okay," she asked.

"Of course," Millie answered.

"I might just stay in there with him actually," Susan continued. "It has been quite a busy day and I think maybe a long winter's nap is just what we both need."

"A long winter's nap can certainly be a kind of magic," Millie agreed. Susan smiled and carried Davy down the hallway as Millie watched them go. *Yes*, she thought to herself, *a long winter's nap is sometimes just exactly the thing a person needs.* As if in response the fireplace blazed up and crackled and for the first time since summer, Millie sighed a sigh of contentment. *Merry Christmas to all, she thought.* And then, *Merry Christmas, Hank.* Millie leaned back into the buttery soft, comfortable couch and closed her eyes, just for a minute.

A Rose By Another Name

By:

Kathryn Haueisen

Author Kathryn Haueisen

Kathryn Haueisen loves to meet fascinating people and write articles and books about them. Sometimes she lets her imagination run wild and writes short stories about imaginary people, loosely based on people she's met. She published six books, is working on book seven, and has published numerous articles in assorted publications. She blogs weekly at:

www.howwisethen.com

A Rose by Another Name

"**A** rose by any other name would smell as sweet."
(William Shakespeare)

Nathan Rose, age 57, rode his bicycle the ten-mile commute from his rural home into town to his office as part of his efforts to do his part to save the planet. Neither rain nor excessive sun deterred him, as long as temperatures ranged between above freezing and less than three digits. On that fateful November day, the temperature was a balmy 60 degrees, with sunny skies when he rode into work. With Christmas fast approaching, he was putting in more overtime hours than usual. He was determined to clear the work calendar to spend more time with his wife, Marie, on her school holiday break.

That day he had worked later than he intended, so he debated about riding his bike back home. It was already starting to get dark. Through the office window he observed ominous clouds forming. He considered Plan B, which consisted of leaving his bike chained to a pole in the parking garage and calling Marie to come fetch him.

If I call Marie, we could do a little Christmas shopping on the way home. But I really need the exercise after sitting in this office all day. It's not that far. Marie is probably exhausted after the kind of days she's been having at school lately. I can probably beat the rain, and even if I don't, I'm waterproof. His decision made, he cleaned up his desk, saved the documents he'd been working on, and put his computer to sleep for the night.

Amanda last saw Bridgetown thirty years ago, when she was about to start going to public school. That year her mother moved her five hundred miles away and never looked back. Most of what Amanda knew about Bridgetown, she learned from her mother's sister, Aunt Sophie. Aunt Sophie lived alone in a wonderful old Victorian style home, with a large wrap-around porch. Or at least, that is how she described her Bridgetown home to Amanda on her yearly visits to see Amanda and her mother. Amanda thought she could remember the house, but she wasn't sure. Amanda tried to imagine what the town would look like. Her memories were sketchy at best. *I remember Mom saying we had to move so I wouldn't have to explain to the other school kids why I didn't have a father. That doesn't really add up. My father died in a car accident, so why would it be a problem that he was gone? And why does she always get so evasive when I ask her about him. Even Aunt Sophie changes the subject when I ask about it. That is odd because Aunt Sophie loves to tell me stories about other people in the family; people I've never met. Perhaps this time, now that I am all grown up and Mom isn't with me, she'll fill me in on my father.*

Bridgetown was named for the bridge that connected the rolling, rural portion of the county to the thirty thousand or so folks who lived in the thriving small city on the hill across the river. Being unfamiliar with the roads leading into town, Amanda took time to pre-set the rental car guidance system for Aunt Sophie's home before she started her drive.

Aunt Sophie had begged her to come for a visit. "I can't come to you anymore. This confounded arthritis is making me a home body, and I do not like it one bit! Come visit your old aunt while I still have me wits about me enough to enjoy our time. 'Tis is where you started your life. I can show you the highlights."

I wonder if anyone ever won an argument with her. Amanda knew she wouldn't when her aunt reminded her that she'd already said she had a long break between editing projects at the small publishing company where she worked. She chuckled as she pictured her aunt sitting on her front porch, wrapped in a quilt, sipping hot herbal tea, and watching for the cherry red Prius Amanda had told her aunt she would be driving. She saw a sign for Route 15 and looked down at her map app to verify that is where she should turn.

Uh oh. I hope it's not much further. I don't like the looks of those clouds.

The rain started just as Nathan was approaching the bridge. He stopped long enough to pull the hood of his slicker over his head. Then, with his head ducked down low in a futile effort to keep the rain from making his glasses useless, he forged ahead. *Over the bridge and through the woods and then only another few miles. I can make it. Marie will no doubt have a hot toddy ready for me.*

The rain started in earnest as Amanda followed Route 15 through the rolling hills toward the bridge. *This really is lovely. I must ask Aunt Sophie to give me the grand tour in daylight when it's not*

raining. Her playlist got to one of her favorite songs and she started tapping her fingers on the steering wheel, straining a bit to see through the rain. She managed to find the rental car windshield wiper and set it on its fastest speed.

The rain began coming down in torrents as Nathan biked slowly across the bridge. *Perhaps I should try to call Marie, but I'll probably ruin the phone if I pull it out now. It's not lightening, and I'm so close. I'll be better off just getting soaked and get home.*

Amanda could no longer hear her song for the sound of rain pounding the Prius roof. Nor could she see more than a few feet in front of her. Route 15 started its windy descent toward the bridge. She gripped the steering wheel tighter, murmured a pray for help, and forged ahead.

At that same time Nathan crossed the bridge and got off his bike to walk it up the steep incline. He was staring down at the ground and pushing his bike gingerly up the hill on Route 15. Amanda approached another curve and leaned in closer to the windshield, trying to figure out where the road was. It was raining so hard she wasn't sure if she was still on the road. As she drove into the curve, she felt something, more than she saw or heard anything. She slammed on the breaks and tried to see through the windshield, but it was hopeless. She couldn't see beyond the front of the car.

Was it a deer? Aunt Sophie warned me they sometimes jump in front of cars. Should I call her? Or maybe 911? Is there reception here? Maybe I should roll down the window and call out? No, I'd be soaked in seconds. Back up?

She decided she'd have to get out of the car and get wet. She took off her glasses and set them on the dashboard. Then she decided to leave her shoes in the car as well. At least she could finish the trip in dry shoes. The instant she opened the door she was drenched, but she hardly noticed because she saw a man lying on the ground with a bicycle on top of him. "Oh my God! Oh no! Oh my God!"

She bent down and cautiously touched him. No response. She watched to see if his chest went up and down, indicating he was breathing, but couldn't tell in the heavy rain. After another long series of "Oh, my God" exclamations, she got back in the car. With trembling hands, she managed to dial 911. It took the emergency operator several minutes to calm her down enough to assess that she'd just hit a bicyclist, did not know if he was dead or alive, and was on Route 15 near the bridge into town.

Amanda hung up and started sobbing. A few minutes later she saw the lights of the ambulance through the gray, rain-saturated sky. A police car followed the ambulance, both speeding toward her. While the ambulance crew tended to Nathan, the police office quizzed Amanda. He persuaded her to get her purse and sit in his car out of the rain so she could tell him what happened. Amanda sat in the back seat with her arms wrapped around her drawn up knees, rocking back and forth. "I didn't see him. I never saw him. I'm . . . I'm. . . I'm so sorry. I never saw him. Oh, my God, did I kill him?"

Eventually the police officer determined it was a most unfortunate accident, attributed to the heavy rain and her lack of familiarity with the route she was driving, in a car that was new to her. "It could have happened to anyone, Miss. Is there someone I should call for you?"

Between sobs and "Oh my, God, I never saw him!" statements, Amanda managed to retrieve her phone and find Aunt Sophie's contact information. Before he could call Amanda's aunt, the ambulance driver reported that Nathan was alive, but unconscious and in pretty rough shape.

The police officer sent out a call to have someone retrieve Nathan's bicycle. Then he called Sophie and assured her that her niece was alright, but in no condition to drive. He called for backup to drive Amanda's car while he took Amanda to Sophie's home. Within a quarter hour a very shaken Amanda was in her aunt's arms.

With Sophie looking over Amanda's shaking shoulders, the police officer said there would be no ticket or charges. "The whole incident was due to the weather. Nobody could have seen anything in those conditions. Nathan was foolish to ride his bike tonight. Gotta admire his devotion to saving the earth, but it nearly put him six feet into it."

"Agreed," said Sophie. "Thanks for getting Amanda to me. Do you think it would be alright if we called the hospital tomorrow to see how Nathan's doing? He was one of my students years ago when I taught high school English. A fine young man, even if he is a bit zealous about the bike riding."

"I'll ask the hospital staff to take your call. I have to stop by there anyway to confirm Nathan's condition for my report. I suggest you put this one to bed."

It took Sophie hours of patient applications of hot tea, wine, sleeping aids, and persistent reminders that it was an accident before Amanda finally dozed off into a few restless hours of sleep.

Early the next morning Sophie called the hospital. The report was grim. Nathan was alive, but in serious condition. He had multiple broken bones, a concussion, and had lost a good deal of blood. The hospital staff had put him into an induced coma until they could get the x-rays and MRI they needed to assess his condition. "One thing is for sure," Sophie told Amanda. "He's going to need a lot of donor blood."

"Will you take me to the hospital to see if they can use my blood? I have to do something. I feel sick about what happened."

A few hours later the hospital called Sophie. When she got off the phone, she turned to Amanda who was eager to know if her blood might help the poor man. "Sit down. Amanda, you are not going to believe what I am about to tell you. And I am so sorry that this will be the way you learn it. Yes, they can use your blood, to help...your father."

Amanda wrinkled her eyebrows. "My father? That's impossible. My father died in another car accident, thirty-five years ago."

"That is what your mother always told you. It seemed easier, less humiliating, than the truth. I urged her to tell you the truth when you were old enough to handle it. But she was afraid you would hate her, and she couldn't bear the thought of losing you. She married your stepfather almost immediately after you moved away from Bridgetown. He was happy to accept you as his own daughter and accepted your mother's story about your birth father's death. She never told Nathan that he was a father. She never told me either. All I ever got from her was that she met a great guy at her summer job and was expecting his baby.

"Our parents were furious. They kicked her out of the house and refused to finance any more of her college education. She came to live with me. This is the house you came home to from the hospital. I watched you some when your mother was at work or in classes. When I couldn't take care of you, Mrs. Greentree across the street kept you."

"I think I remember her! Did she have a dog? A brown dog with long curly fur?"

"She did. A lovely Cocker Spaniel that you adored. You can be mighty proud of your mother, Amanda. She earned the money she needed to finish college and transferred to the community college here. It took her almost until you were ready to start school to graduate, but she did it."

"Did your parents ever forgive her? Did they ever meet me?"

Sophie slowly shook her head and sighed deeply. "No. I kept trying to get them to see the blessing that you were and overlook how and when you were conceived. But they refused to even let me bring you to meet them. The one time I tried, while your mother was at work, they slammed the door in my face and told me I was as sinful as she was for harboring the two of you."

Amanda chewed on her fingernails, a habit she'd all but given up until this news hit her with the force of a gale wind.

"So that's why I never met any of my grandparents. Mom always just told me they lived very far away. But I'm confused. So, I'm not really Amanda Carter? I'm really Amanda...Amanda what? What is Nathan's last name?"

"Rose. Nathan Rose. And yes, you really are Amanda Carter. John Carter legally adopted you when he married my sister Sarah. Nathan Rose had no idea you existed, well until you ran into him yesterday."

Amanda burst into tears. Sophie apologized. "I'm sorry dear, that was bad form on my part. You'd think an English teacher could have phrased that a little more delicately. Nathan, your father, is married to a wonderful woman named Marie. They had only one child. A little girl. The poor little thing died from a childhood disease that isn't supposed to be fatal, but in her case, it was."

Amanda chewed on this information, along with her nails for a while. Then she stood up and announced, "I want to meet him."

"And I'm sure he'll want to meet you. But he's in a coma, remember? He needs a transfusion. I think our next move is to take you back to the hospital to donate some blood."

Three days later Sophie led Amanda into Room 406. They found Nathan propped up in bed, with bandages, casts, and tubes everywhere. A middle-aged woman was on the far side of the bed stroking the part of Nathan's arm that wasn't in a cast.

Sophie decided it was her task to navigate this first encounter. "Marie, Nathan, I'd like to introduce you to my niece, Amanda. Amanda is the woman who donated her blood for your transfusion."

"Thank you, thank you, thank you. How can we ever thank you enough?" asked Marie.

"Yes, what my wife said," agreed Nathan.

"Don't thank me too much," said Amanda. "I'm also the woman who ran into you. I'm so sorry. I just couldn't see you in all that rain."

"Well, young lady, don't be too hard on yourself. As I've already been told, numerous times, in a variety of creative ways," Nathan said as he looked at Marie, "I should have never tried to ride my bike in that storm. Lesson learned!"

Sophie went on. "Nathan, I'm glad you're already lying down. Marie, you may want to sit down in that chair."

This was met with quizzable looks, but Marie did as Sophie suggested.

Sophie took in a very deep breath, wrapped her arm around Amanda's shoulder, and announced, "Nathan, meet your daughter, Amanda Carter."

Nathan stared, with his chin nearly on his chest. Marie shrieked and jumped to her feet. Then everyone tried to talk all at once, until a nurse came in to check Nathan's vitals and an awkward silence fell over the room.

When the nurse left, Sophie resumed. "Marie, Nathan never knew about Amanda. It was a short-term college summer fling that ended before Amanda's mother, my sister Sarah, even knew she was pregnant. Our parents kicked her out and cut her off financially. She came to stay with me. I tried to suggest she either get an abortion or insist the father help pay her expenses. She was adamant about two things. She would not get an abortion and she would never tell either Nathan or Amanda about the circumstances of her birth.

"I knew about the summer romance, but Sarah would never tell me who her secret summer lover was. I'm as shocked as you. Please don't be too hard on Nathan. He and my sister were college kids with more hormones than brains at the time."

Nathan turned red and stared down at the bed control on his lap.

"And Nathan, I am so very sorry this is how you found out. Sarah believed with all her heart, and mind, and even soul, that she was doing the right thing at the time. She didn't want you to marry her under that kind of pressure. And she didn't want you to change your career plans. She let Amanda grow up believing you died in a car accident before she was born. She married a really decent man a few years later. Together they've given Amanda a pretty good life."

The silence returned while each person tried to digest this news and decide what to do with it. Marie was the first to break the silence. "Come here, Amanda. I guess this makes me your stepmother. Perhaps Sophie already told you. We lost our little girl Gail years ago. I was never able to have another baby and we never got around to adopting. Do you think your mother would let you spend Christmas with us?"

Amanda accepted the hug her stepmother offered and nodded her head. She pulled back, wiped her running nose with the back of her hand, and through her tears said, "I'll ask her."

Then Amanda turned to Nathan, "I'm so sorry I hit you! But, in a way, I'm kinda glad too, since you know, you're gonna live. 'Cause if I hadn't hit you, they wouldn't have tested our blood and I might never have met you."

Nathan motioned with his one good arm to come closer. He pulled her in for a hug, then pushed her away so he could look at her. "I remember that summer. It was intense, but we both understood it was a summer romance. We met at the resort where we worked. Once the summer ended and I went back to school, I never saw or heard from your mother again. I think about her every once in a while, but I didn't have any idea of where she was, or how to find her again. I had no idea she was pregnant.

"Do you mind if I call you Amanda Rose? It would mean a lot to me to have you use my name some of the time. Perhaps as a middle name? Or a nickname I could call you? I don't mean anything that requires a trip to the courthouse or anything. I just like the sound of it. Amanda Rose. I like how that sounds. Do you mind?"

"It's OK by me. If you don't mind if I call you Dad. Deal?"

"Deal."

When Sophie and Amanda got back to Sophie's home they debated how, when and if they should fill Amanda's mother in on the events in Bridgetown.

"I kinda get it," admitted Amanda. "If I had a baby I wasn't expecting, I'm not sure I'd want to get all tangled up with the guy for the rest of my life. But I wish she trusted me enough to tell me the truth."

"Things were different back then. Men came and went as they pleased. But if a girl got pregnant, she could pretty much write off her future. Moving away and saying your father was killed in an accident got her pity. The truth would have gotten her public shaming and isolation. It was rough enough those first few years until she met your stepfather."

"Well, I have to let her know that I know. How do you propose we do that?"

"I could invite them to come for Christmas."

"And I could just casually mention that I'll need to leave for a few hours to go visit my dad."

"And after she comes too from passing out, we could tell her how you met him."

In the end, they decided a conference call now was a better idea than springing such news on Sarah Christmas Day. Amanda told her mother about the car accident and promised her mother she was OK, and so was the man she hit.

She then let Sophie explain about how Amanda met her birth father.

"Please, come for Christmas. I promise you; Nathan is thrilled to know he has a daughter. Marie is equally happy to have a step-daughter. They're lovely people. And for the record, I am very pleased that Nathan Rose is the father of my niece. He's a good man, Sarah."

Nathan started the round of cheers over Christmas Dinner. "To my good fortune at being run over by this delightful young lady, who turns out to be the daughter I never knew I had."

Sophie raised her glass high. "Praise to the Lord whose birth we celebrate this day, that at last we all know the truth about Amanda's birth.

Marie took her turn. "How miraculous that an actual car accident corrects the myth about a made-up story of another accident and brings us together. I don't know what they call the relationship between women who have shared the same man, and also share a daughter, but I think the right word should be 'family.'"

Sarah stood, cleared her throat, coughed, and said, "To Sophie for inviting Amanda to visit. To you, my dear husband, for filling in all these years as Amanda's father. And to you, Nathan and Marie, for welcoming us into your lives."

John looked into the face of everyone gathered around the table, and announced, "God bless us, everyone."

Amanda got in the final word, "I'm pretty sure God just did."

The Year Christmas Came Early

By:

LM Mann

Author LM Mann

Author, Entrepreneur, Media Producer

LM Mann (Lydia) has a passion for working with children. For over 30 years, she has worked with summer camps across the USA producing videos. She has coached children in basketball and soccer programs through her church and conducted creative writing workshops with schools and camps.

Lydia hopes to inspire young readers to develop a passion for reading as she did as a child. *"It is extremely important to help children develop a love of reading. Reading allows children not only to do better in school, but instills a love of learning, and supports their natural curiosity. I still remember the magic moment when my dad was reading me the same book that he had to read me every night before bed, when I realized I was actually reading the words on my own."*

Two of her books have won multiple awards.

"I'm honored by the acclaim, but the best reward is a kid who tells me, 'I loved your book!'."

You can find her at:

https://mannwrites.com/

The Year Christmas Came Early

〜

T o all those horse-crazy kids (and adults) who always wanted a horse for Christmas.

"Mr. Klein, what would you take for that horse?" asked the girl. Her heart raced, as she hoped harder than she had ever hoped in her entire nine years of life.

...weeks earlier.

School was out for the summer. With both her parents working, Ismay (Izzy to her friends) took turns hanging out with her dad, who remodeled houses. Her mom's job as a nurse did not allow her to tag along to the local hospital. Her Aunt Rosa was on a month long vacation, so she could not stay with her. Going with Poppy, as she called her dad, was the plan for the coming weeks.

Poppy was helping a local rancher remodel a home on his

property. Izzy looked forward to being her dad's helper for a while.

Poppy pulled onto a gravel drive. Izzy jumped out of the dusty red pickup truck to open the ranch gate.

"Shut it behind us," said Poppy. "We don't want Mr. Klein's cattle getting out."

"Yes, sir," she answered, as she waved him through. After closing the gate, she hopped back into the truck for the short drive to the house Poppy would be working on.

A tall man with a broad smile waved in greeting. He wore a straw cowboy hat and work worn boots. He stepped out of the front door to shake hands with Poppy.

"Howdy, David. Who's the new supervisor?" The rancher nodded and winked at Izzy.

Poppy smiled. "Mr. Klein, this is my daughter, Ismay. She's the one I told you about."

"Nice to meet you, Ismay," he tipped his hat, and then he reached out to shake her hand.

"Nice to meet you, sir," she took his hand. She felt the work-hardened calluses, as the rancher's large hand engulfed hers. "You can call me Izzy, everybody does," she tried to remember to shake his hand firmly and look him in the eye, just like Poppy taught her.

"Welcome to Lazy K Ranch, Izzy," he replied. He released her hand and motioned to the large pastures that seemed to go on forever. "We have a couple of stock tanks over there," he pointed toward a rolling green meadow. "You're welcome to go fishing, if you get bored helping us two old guys." He smiled again.

"That's very kind of you," said Poppy. "If you go out to the pastures, be careful around the herd. Don't spook them," her dad cautioned.

"Yes, sir," she replied.

"Those cows are pretty used to people," said Mr. Klein. "Just let them know you're around. There's also a chestnut mare out there with them. She's a sweet horse that someone abandoned.

I've been feeding her and letting her run with my cows, until I figure out what to do with her."

'A horse!?!' thought Izzy, 'This just got a whole lot more exciting!'

It took a couple of hours helping Poppy and Mr. Klein before Izzy was able to get permission to go exploring. The number one goal – find the horse!

Izzy saw the herd of cows at the crest of a hill. It overlooked a stock pond with several trees along the bank. She headed toward the herd at a fast walk. As much as she wanted to run, she did not want to scare the cows and their babies.

She slowed her pace when she was within a hundred yards of the closest cow. The cow was content to munch the lush grass, as her large calf played nearby.

"Hello, momma cows," Izzy said, stopping her progress to make sure the herd knew she was getting close. "My name is Izzy. I just wanted to come say hello."

The cattle raised their heads and looked the girl over. Since she was not a threat, nor did she have a feed bucket in her hand, they quickly went back to grazing.

"Any of you ladies seen a brown horse around here?" the girl asked. Since none of them seemed interested, she walked on, skirting the edge of the herd.

"Your girl okay with livestock," asked Mr. Klein, watching out the window as the girl approached the herd. His concern reflected on his face.

"Absolutely," Izzy's dad replied, noting the direction of the rancher's gaze. "She's a regular Dr. Doolittle, my Izzy," he chuckled. "By the end of the week, she'll probably have all your cows following her around like a bunch of puppies."

The rancher smiled at the thought.

"Our steers, chickens, and two nanny goats, think she's just one of the herd," David laughed. "And don't get me started about the two ranch dogs and three barn cats!"

The two men laughed.

"She sounds a lot like my girl at that age," said the rancher. "I made the mistake of letting her raise bunnies for a 4-H project when she was nine. Those dang rabbits lived until she was a college junior."

The two fathers chuckled, both proud of the daughters they were blessed to have.

Izzy's heart sang as she spotted the chestnut mare. She was grazing a little way off from the cows, near the bottom of the hill. In Izzy's eyes, she was the most beautiful horse she had ever seen. She had a thin, white blaze down her face. Her mane and tail were black, and three of her four legs had white stockings up to her knees. She might as well have stepped out of one of the horse books Izzy read by the dozen.

"Hi, pretty girl," Izzy said softly. The girl walked slowly toward the horse, carefully watching the horse's body language. "My name is Ismay, but everybody calls me Izzy," she continued. "I wonder what your name is?"

Izzy stopped a few yards away from the horse. She knew not to crowd her. She wanted to let the horse decide the next step.

The horse had her ears forward. She seemed curious about the girl. As she finished munching a mouthful of grass, she wandered towards the girl.

"That's it, pretty girl. I just want to be friends."

The horse stopped just out of reach. Izzy stood still for another minute. She was so excited, she wanted to jump up and down. But Poppy taught her that horses, and most animals, responded best to calm energy.

When Izzy could not stand it another second, she took a step forward. The horse turned her head away. Izzy stopped and took a step back. She knew letting the horse decide to engage on her terms would help build respect and trust between the two of them. Izzy stood still, trying to project calmness and positive energy.

"It's okay, girl, I won't rush you."

The horse's natural curiosity broke the stalemate. She turned her head toward the girl and snorted a friendly snort.

"Will you come to me, or you want me to come to you?" Izzy asked, watching the horse's body language. She seemed relaxed. Her ears were forward, and she looked the girl in the eye.

"Okay, let's try again," she stepped forward. This time Pretty Girl, as Izzy had already named the mare, reached out and nuzzled the girl's outstretched hand.

"Poppy, do you think it would be okay to take a brush with me today? I want to try to groom Pretty Girl," Izzy asked, as she and her dad finished loading the pickup.

He smiled. "Pretty Girl?"

The girl blushed. "Well, I can't just call her *Horse*."

Poppy chuckled and muffed the top of her head with affection. "I suppose that's true. Well, why don't you take one with you and ask Mr. Klein. We have to respect that she is his horse."

"Oh, yes, sir," she quickly agreed. "It's really nice of him to let me make friends with her." She stuck the brush, along with a few carrots into her backpack.

After arriving at the ranch, it did not take Izzy long to ask Mr. Klein about grooming Pretty Girl.

"That would be fine, Izzy," the rancher replied, "but it would be safer if you had her tied up while you groom her."

Izzy nodded respectfully.

"I've got an old halter and lead rope in the barn. I'll grab it when we break for lunch. Then you and I can go try it on that mare. Okay?" The rancher smiled.

"That would be great!" she replied. "She hasn't been fussy at all when I handle her head. I just know she will be good with a halter," she explained.

"Well, after lunch, we will give it a try," he said, smiling at the girl's enthusiasm.

"Thank you, sir," said Izzy, as she raced out the door to plead with Pretty Girl to behave after lunch.

Izzy called to Pretty Girl as she and Mr. Klein walked across the pasture. The horse snorted a friendly greeting, curious about the visit from the girl and rancher.

"Howdy, girl," Mr. Klein said as he shook the feed bucket he carried. "Let's see how you're going to do with a halter."

The horse approached confidently. Her attention focused more on the feed bucket than the halter.

"Izzy, you hold the bucket, and I'll see if I can slip this on her head."

"Here you go, Pretty Girl. Have a snack," she told the horse.

Mr. Klein slipped the halter on the horse with dexterity that came from years of experience. Pretty Girl hardly noticed as she munched her oats.

"You're such a good girl," Izzy praised the mare.

"Yes, she is," said the rancher, handing Izzy the lead rope. He patted the mare's neck affectionately. "You two have a good time this afternoon. Me and your dad have to get back to work."

"Thank you so much, Mr. Klein," she said, giving the tall rancher a quick hug.

He smiled and affectionately tussled her hair.

Izzy led Pretty Girl to a nearby tree. The shade was appreciated by both girl and horse. Izzy set the feed bucket next to the tree and tied the lead rope around the trunk. She gave the horse enough rope to still reach the mostly empty bucket.

The girl pulled the brush out of her backpack and got to work. Pretty Girl basked in the attention. Izzy bushed and brushed removing all the dried mud out of the horse's mane. The dirt and dander that had accumulated over time blew away in the gentle breeze as each stroke of the brush moved across the horse's back and sides.

Both girl and horse sneezed a few times. Izzy laughed.

"You want to take a carrot break?" she asked. Pretty Girl's ears twitched at the word carrot.

The girl retrieved the snack from her backpack. She snapped the carrot into several pieces, then offered a bite on her flattened outstretched palm. Pretty Girl's soft lips tickled as she took the proffered morsel from the girl. The horse munched appreciatively.

Seeing the beauty emerge from months of dirt on Pretty Girl's coat was worth all the sweat and effort.

"I should have brought a hoof pick," Izzy said, picking up the horse's front hoof, pleasantly surprised at the ease at which she did so. She knew that some horses were extremely fussy about their feet, but Pretty Girl cooperated on the first try. She bent over examining the horse's hoof while cradling it in her hand.

"I'll see if I can find one tonight at home or see if Dad will let me have a screwdriver." She released the leg and stood up straight. Pretty Girl shifted her weight back to all four feet, then reached over to nuzzle the girl.

Izzy hugged the horse as she said, "You really are a pretty girl. I wish you were mine."

"Poppy? You know how every Christmas I put a horse on the top of my list for Santa?" she asked, earnestly looking at her dad as he drove.

'Oh boy,' he thought, *'here we go.'* "I seem to remember that is a reoccurring theme," he answered.

"You know I'm nine now. I'm big enough to take care of a horse," the girl explained.

"Uh huh," her dad mused, slightly dreading the rest of the conversation.

"Pretty Girl's previous owner didn't want her. Can you even imagine?!" the girl still incredulous at the thought. "Mr. Klein has been really nice to look after her, but his daughter is off at college. She can't look after a horse, and Mr. Klein is too busy to ride her," the girl plowed on. "She's just stuck out there wandering around with the cows." Izzy made her case better than any courtroom lawyer.

"Are you leading up to what I think you are?" asked Poppy.

The girl smiled anxiously. "I guess I am. Poppy can we buy Pretty Girl? Maybe Mr. Klein won't ask too much for her."

"Well, Izzy, if you want that mare, you're going to have to ask Mr. Klein yourself. Depending on his price, your mom and I will think about it."

The girl's face turned serious. "Okay, I'll ask him in the morning."

Izzy hardly slept that night. When she did sleep, her dreams alternated between Pretty Girl grazing in her back pasture, or being taken away forever by some unknown person. She awoke early, tired from excitement and worry.

"You're up early," her mom said, as Izzy walked into the kitchen.

"I couldn't sleep very well," said the girl. "Mom, what if Mr. Klein says he won't sell Pretty Girl?" Izzy asked, sitting next to her mom at the kitchen table.

"That's his decision, Izzy," her mom explained. "We have to be ready to accept it."

The girl sighed. "I know."

"We also have to be ready to accept that the price may be too high," her mom continued. "Your father and I work hard to provide a good life for our family, but we don't have a whole lot for extras."

"I know, Mom," she said, trying to be brave.

Izzy and her dad pulled into the driveway of Lazy K Ranch. Izzy was determined to be grown up about the situation. She would be brave, no matter what Mr. Klein decided, she promised herself.

Poppy leaned cross the front seat and gave her an encouraging pat on the knee.

"Good luck, kiddo." He smiled. "Now go do some horse tradin'."

Izzy jumped down from the truck. She squared her shoulders and walked up to greet the rancher sitting in the shade of the front porch.

"Good morning, Miss Izzy," he said with a smile.

"Good morning, Mr. Klein. Can I ask you an important question?" she asked.

Her dad watched from the back of the pickup. He pretended to be busy getting his tools.

"Well, sure thing, Izzy. What's on your mind?"

"Mr. Klein, what would you take for that horse?" Izzy nodded toward the pasture. She almost forgot to breathe. She hoped harder than she had ever hoped in her nine years of life.

The rancher smiled and said, "You really have taken a shine to that little ole mare, haven't you?"

"Yes, sir. She's the best horse ever."

Poppy walked up behind her, offering silent encouragement with his presence.

"David," Mr. Klein looked up to her dad, "your girl wants to buy that horse. You okay with her horse trading with me?" He smiled.

"I suppose so," Poppy replied. "I told her if she was going to be in the horse business, she had to do her own negotiations."

The men exchanged a knowing glance, while Izzy tried to be patient.

"Well, Izzy, I need to talk to my wife before I can make a decision. I will talk to her tonight and let you know in the morning. That work for you?" the rancher asked.

"Okay," Izzy replied. "Thank you, sir."

"I guess you better head out to the pasture and give that mare a good brushing." He winked.

"I will!" She practically stood at attention before racing out to see Pretty Girl.

"She's a sweet kid, David," the rancher said to her dad.

"Thanks, Marcus. I don't have to tell you that she's crazy about that horse." He laughed.

"Let me talk to the wife. We'll come up with a fair price for you guys."

"Thanks. I have cautioned Izzy that we have a budget. We have to be fair to everyone involved."

"She's a good kid. We'll figure something out."

The two men grabbed their tool belts and got to work on the house.

"Pretty Girl, I asked Mr. Klein if I could buy you," Izzy explained, as she brushed the chestnut's silky neck. "It would be the best thing EVER, if you can be my horse."

The horse seemed to agree.

"We could help Poppy when he needs to count cows. We could even try barrel racing if you like it. Best of all, we will be together FOREVER."

That evening over dinner the Kleins discussed Izzy and the horse.

"I was thinking $1000 would be a fair price for that mare. She can't be more than seven or eight years old. She's healthy, sound feet, and gentle enough for that little girl," he told his wife.

She gave him "the look." The one she gave him when he was in trouble.

"What?" he asked, wondering where he went wrong.

"How much did you pay for that horse?" she asked.

He somehow knew he was not going to make a profit on this deal. "Nothing."

"You are going to give that sweet girl that horse, Marcus Klein. Every horse-crazy kid deserves their own horse."

He chuckled, knowing she was right.

After another restless night, Izzy joined her parents at the breakfast table.

"Your mom and I have been discussing things," Poppy said, as she slid into her chair at the kitchen table. "We can afford up to $1000 for Pretty Girl, but if Mr. Klein needs more than that, we will have to walk away from the deal."

Izzy nodded, her emotions swirling. She sipped her juice as she tried to steady her nerves.

"We know you really want her, Baby, but..." her mom smiled and shrugged.

"I know," Izzy said quietly. "Thanks. I just really, really hope we can get her."

Izzy tried not to run after hopping down out of her dad's pickup. *'If I have to wait much longer, 'I might just have a heart attack,'* she thought.

Mr. Klein waited for her and Poppy on the front porch, his hat slightly cocked back, a cup of coffee in one hand. He smiled at the girl's obvious excitement.

"Well, Miss Izzy," he said, as she and her dad joined him on the front porch, "I suppose we have a little horse tradin' to do this morning."

"Yes, sir," she replied, determined to be brave.

"That mare is a good horse," he continued, "but horses are a big responsibility."

The girl nodded in agreement.

"If you were to get her, I would need to know that you are ready to take good care of her. You would need to muck her stall, groom her, and check her feet regularly. Owning a horse is more than just throwing a saddle on and going for a ride when you feel like it."

Poppy nodded in agreement.

"Yes, sir," she agreed. "I promise I will take really good care of her."

The rancher smiled. "Well, I had a feeling you would agree with all of that. You have taken good care of her just while she's been out in my pasture."

"Thank you, sir."

"Since that is the case, me and the missus have decided to give you that mare, Izzy. She deserves to be loved by a sweet girl like you."

Izzy could not believe what she just heard. "You mean give her to me, like a present?"

"Yup," he chuckled. "I guess Christmas came a little early this year."

"Oh, thank you!" She threw her arms around the tall rancher. He knelt to receive the embrace. "Thank you so much, Mr. Klein. Pretty Girl is the best present EVER!"

"You're welcome, Izzy," his heart warmed by her innocent joy.

The trip home that afternoon included a stop by the farm store. Izzy's dad chuckled as his daughter agonized over choosing the perfect halter and lead rope.

"Do you think Pretty Girl would like pink or purple better?" she asked her dad.

"I'm not sure, Izzy. Do you think she'll really care?"

"Daaaad... of course she'll care!" the girl responded, incredulous.

He laughed gently and said, "Why don't you worry about choosing the right color, while I go grab a couple of bags of feed." He left his daughter looking at halters.

"Maybe blue?" she said, as her dad walked to the horse feed aisle.

The next day, wearing a new pink halter with a pink lead rope, Pretty Girl walked into the back of Poppy's livestock trailer. Izzy's heart nearly burst from excitement. The trip home did not take long.

That evening, after her mom called her to come in from the barn for the third time, Izzy said, "I gotta go, girl." She hugged the horse, *her horse…*one last time for the night.

"Good night, girl. I'll see you in the morning," she said, turning to leave the stall. She stopped, throwing her arms around the horse's neck one more time, "I love you, Pretty Girl. You're my very best friend."

A Chaos Christmas

By
Mandy McCool

Author Mandy McCool

Mandy McCool is a freelance writer, trying to find her big break into published writing. She first started writing poetry at a young age, landing a spot in the *Who's Who Anthology of Poetry* in the fifth grade. She has since moved on to writing short and not so short stories that she shares with her Squad. When she's not using her free time writing, Mandy enjoys going to Texas Rangers baseball games, Renaissance festivals, and Comic-con. This is her first published short story.

Instagram:
https://www.instagram.com/mandymac07/
Facebook:
https://www.facebook.com/mandymac07

A Chaos Christmas

❦

Snow covered the ground along the driving trail Manda had taken to get to the cabin. She was going to be the first to arrive out of the seven women who were coming to stay the next few days. The trail got steeper the farther along she went, until finally it leveled out and Manda could see the cabin the Squad had rented.

The two-story wood structure looked like something straight off a Christmas card. Snow beautifully covered the roof and icicles hung from the railings. The trees surrounding the cabin were lush and green and as she stopped the Jeep and got out, she could smell the aroma of the Evergreen needles.

Manda took a few photos before she headed up the steps to the front door. She took out her phone and found the email the owner had sent that contained the code. After punching it in, she opened the door soundlessly. The front entrance hall was lit, and there was a small gift basket sitting on the side table to her right. She picked up the card and read:

"Welcome, Chaos Squad! We hope your stay at the Christmas Cabin is magical! There are plenty of things for all of you to join in on! Please feel free to use any and all decorations that are located in the shed behind the house. If you have any questions or issues, do not hesitate to reach out!

Merry Christmas!

The Pelznickels"

Smiling, Manda placed the card back on the table. She thought it was really nice of them to let them use the decorations. She would have to go out and check to see what they had, but first, she needed to bring in everything from her car. She trudged back outside and started unloading.

About an hour later, Manda had everything inside and put away except her suitcases. She wanted to wait for the others before deciding on rooms. She knew they were going to have to share rooms and wanted to make sure everyone was happy with the arrangements.

After making a cup of hot tea, Manda sat in one of the large easy chairs with her book to wait on the others. She knew Ma, Ry, and Kass were due first. Fish and Lissa had to go to the airport to pick up B who was flying in from Iceland. As she settled in, she dozed off.

Jumping awake at the sound of a car horn, Manda got up from the chair and walked to the front door. She put her boots back on and walked out onto the front porch. She saw Ry's Jeep pull in followed by Fish's Nissan. As the girls piled out of the cars, Manda waved at them.

"Hey! I thought you guys would be here later!" She said as Lissa came into view.

Ry laughed. "Well, Fish didn't want to get lost, so we waited for them to get B and then they followed us up here."

"Yeah, Fish is directionally challenged," Kass said with a smirk.

Fish slapped Kass on the arm playfully. "I am not! If anything, it's Manda's fault! She's the one that found this place." She had reached the porch and gave Manda a huge hug. "How did you find it, anyway?"

Shrugging, Manda replied, "Honestly, I have no clue. I knew we were discussing getting together to spend Christmas with each other, and the next thing I knew, I received a phone call asking if I was interested in renting the cabin. I thought it was a scam at first, but Mr. Pelznickle met with me and Kass in person."

"Well, it is seriously a beautiful cabin," Ma chimed in. She hugged Manda too before following Fish inside.

Manda moved aside to let the other girls enter. She hugged each of them, except Kass, as they passed. "The owners left a note too. There are decorations and stuff in the shed out back. We can use what we want to really make it feel like Christmas."

"That is so nice of them!" exclaimed B. "We can see who decorates better, Americans or Icelanders."

"Oh! You get to experience an American Christmas!" said Lissa.

Manda smiled. "I think B was going to share some of her traditions as well. I know of one that I think everyone here will enjoy."

"Is it the one where you exchange books on Christmas Eve and spend the day reading them?" asked Fish. When Manda nodded, she continued, "Good! I have just the book I want to share. Who are we exchanging with?"

"I figured we could draw names out of a hat to see who our books will go to," Manda answered.

Everyone looked excited at the prospect of new books. They all moved into the kitchen to discuss who they hoped to get.

"Hey, so what about the sleeping arrangements?" asked Kass. "We should probably unload the cars before it gets dark."

"Well, there are four rooms upstairs. Three of them have two beds in them and one that only has one. I figured we could draw room numbers to see who gets what room."

The Squad nodded in agreement. Manda found a pad of

paper and a pen that was in a drawer. She ripped them into seven pieces and wrote down the room numbers on them. She folded them, dropped them into a cup, and shook it.

"So, who wants to go first?" Manda asked. "Just don't look until everyone has chosen."

B raised her hand quickly. Manda held out the cup and she took a slip. Lissa, Fish, Ma, Kass, and then finally Ry choose theirs. Manda took out the last slip and placed the cup on the island before opening it up.

"I have number three," she said, showing them her slip.

Lissa smiled. "Me too! Guess we are roomies!"

Ry opened hers and saw she was sharing with Fish in room two. B and Kass were going to room together in room four, which meant Ma had the single room to herself.

"Woo! Yes!" Ma said giggling.

"Ever so humble there, Ma," Ry laughed.

Ma stuck her tongue out at her. Manda shook her head at her friends and then motioned them all to follow her back outside. They all started unloading and carrying things inside. Manda helped them all take their bags upstairs to their rooms.

Each double room had two large four-poster beds, a night stand for each bed, and two dressers. Ma's room had a king size bed with a table and dresser. After checking out each other's rooms, the girls all split up to start unpacking. Manda told them that she was going to put pizzas in the oven and that when they were ready, they could come into the kitchen to grab what they wanted.

Manda checked the pizza boxes and preheated both ovens. She was glad the cabin had double ovens so she could slide in all four pizzas at the same time. She then found a Bluetooth radio and hooked her phone to it. She turned on her Christmas playlist and started taking out plates for dinner. She didn't realize it, but she started singing to herself softly.

"Wow, Manda. I didn't know you had such a good voice."

Manda startled. She turned quickly to the door of the

kitchen. "Liss, you scared me! How long have you been standing there?"

Lissa chuckled as she entered the kitchen. "Since about 'six geese a-laying'. But don't worry, I won't tell the others."

"Tell the others what?" Asked Kass as she joined the other two.

"I wasn't paying attention and was singing." Manda answered. "Lissa caught me."

"She does that a lot actually. She never believes me when I tell her she sounds fine," Kass said.

"See? I told you, Manda."

Manda just shook her head at her two friends. The timer on the pizza went off and Manda grabbed the oven mitts and pulled them out. As she grabbed a pizza cutter from the drawer, the rest of the group joined them.

"I could smell the pizza upstairs," Fish said as she tried to steal a pepperoni.

Manda smacked her hand softly. "Manners, Fish."

Fish stuck out her tongue, but then laughed. Manda handed them all a plate and told them to help themselves. They all situated themselves around the table and sat down to eat. The only thing they heard for a few minutes was the music playing softly.

"So," said Ry as she used her crust to point at Manda. "What's on the agenda for the next few days?"

Everyone turned to Manda in anticipation. "Why do I have to have all the answers?"

"Well, for starters, this was your idea. Second, you rented the cabin. And C, you told me you had some stuff planned." Kass smirked at her best friend.

Rolling her eyes with a small smile playing on her lips, Manda relented. "Ok, I may have some stuff planned. Tonight though, I figured we would all be tired from traveling so I have some board games. Tomorrow, we could see what decorations we have and decorate the house. On Friday, I figured we could ride into the little town and go Christmas shopping. Then in the evening, we'll exchange books and a few other traditions. And then Saturday morning, we can exchange gifts and then make a Christmas feast."

"Wow, you haven't thought at all about what we can do together, have you?" Ma laughed, and pretty soon the rest of the Squad had joined in.

"I mean, y'all put me in charge. But if there's anything you wanna do instead, I am all ears."

"It sounds like a solid plan. Spending time together and having a blast. I'm down," Ry said, smiling.

"Same here!" Exclaimed B. "So, what are we gonna play first?"

The rest of the evening the girls played games and laughed until their cheeks hurt. The fire burned lower and lower but no one was quite ready to be the first to go to bed. When B had yawned four times in a row, they decided that they should turn in. Manda cleaned up the cards and placed the lid back on the box. With Lissa's help, she carried the plates from dinner to the kitchen to place them in the dishwasher. She added the pizza pans and cutter and then wiped the counter.

She followed Lissa up the stairs toward their room, and after changing into her pajamas, she stuck her head in Ma's room to tell her goodnight.

"Hey Ma. Just wanted to make sure you were good before bed."

Ma smiled. "Just tired. Today was great. Thank you for finding all this."

"I mean, I just found the cabin. The idea was a shared one." Manda said, leaning on the door jam.

"Still, I am really glad we are all together for Christmas."

"Me too, Ma. Now get some sleep. Love you."

Manda headed back to her room and stopped in the other's rooms to say goodnight and to tell them breakfast would be at ten.

Lissa was snoring lightly when she got back to their room. Manda climbed into bed and smiled to herself. She really was glad they got to be together for Christmas.

The next morning dawned bright and early. Manda woke when her alarm went off and turned it off quickly. She didn't want to wake Lissa. She got up and headed down to the kitchen.

She started the coffee pot, and then started pulling out the things she needed for breakfast. Ry wandered into the kitchen as she was looking for the griddle.

"Morning, Manda! What's for breakfast?"

"Pancakes, eggs, and bacon. I just can't seem to find a griddle."

Ry helped Manda search the cabinets. "What about waffles instead?"

Manda turned and saw Ry pulling out a waffle maker. "That'll work! Waffles are better anyway. Thanks Ry!"

Her friend beamed. She set to work mixing the batter while Manda started heating up the pan to fry the bacon.

"Wonder what kind of eggs everyone likes?" Manda asked out loud.

Ry shrugged. "You could just scramble them all so it would be easier to cook. Or you could wait for everyone to come downstairs and ask."

"I'll just scramble some," Manda said. "If they want them a different way, I can always make them a couple."

The girls talked about Christmas and their excitement as they cooked breakfast together. Manda really liked being able to decorate the house, and Ry was ready to show B how they decorated a tree.

The rest of the Squad trickled down as they woke and showered. Fish was first and she helped set the table with plates and silverware. Kass joined not long after and grabbed the condiments. Ma and Lissa were next and they helped carry the platters of warm food to the table. B was last, and when she sat down, her face split into a giant yawn.

Kass laughed. "Aw, poor B. She's a sweepy wittle bug."

B gave Kass an annoyed look. It made her disheveled look even funnier. "You try to change four time zones and actually get enough sleep."

"It's totally fine," Manda said, interjecting. "Maybe knowing we are decorating today will help you feel more awake."

B's eyes widened. "Oh, yes! I do want to decorate!"

"So, are we doing the outside and the inside?" asked Lissa. She took a huge bite of waffle and dripped syrup on her shirt.

Manda chuckled as she handed her friend a napkin. "Depends on what kind of decorations there are in the shed. But hopefully there will be enough for both."

The Squad nodded excitedly. They all quickly finished breakfast. Ma told Manda and Ry to go get showered and dressed while the rest of them cleaned up from breakfast. It was the least they could do since Manda and Ry had cooked it all.

About an hour later, the Squad had shrugged on their coats and headed out to the shed to see what they had. The inside was bigger than it looked on the outside and Manda could tell they had plenty of decorations for both inside and outside.

"So, since we can do both, maybe we should divide and conquer. The tree we can all do this evening. Who wants what?" She asked.

"I want to be inside!" said B. "I feel like I would fall off a ladder trying to put lights on the house."

Manda laughed. "I mean, same. But I think outside would be fun."

Lissa and Ma decided to help B inside, while Fish, Ry, and Kass all said they'd help Manda. They started grabbing the crates with the lights and other Christmassy things, and started taking them back to the house.

"Hey, so what about a small wager?" Fish asked, a glint in her eyes. "Best decorators get first dibs on showers tomorrow morning. Losers have to make breakfast."

B squinted at Fish before smirking. "I'll take that bet. I know Lissa, Ma and I got this in the bag."

"Sure you do, B," clapped back Kass.

Ry cracked her knuckles and nodded in agreement.

Manda and Ma just laughed at their friends. The groups separated and Manda opened up a crate of colored lights. She started pulling them out and noticed that they were wrapped neatly so they weren't tangled. "This is going to be a piece of cake."

The next couple hours, and a few smashed fingers later, Manda and Fish had all the lights on the front of the house. They covered the roof and all along the porch railings. Icicle lights hung from the handrails on the stairs. Fish stood back to admire their work. Manda connected the light plugs together.

"Maybe we should wait to turn them on until it gets dark," Manda said. "It would make the effect much better so we can win."

Fish nodded. "I agree. Besides, I don't want the Insiders to see them. Let's go check on Kass and Ry."

The two stepped off the porch and turned toward the sound of a commotion.

"No, Ry! That doesn't go like that!"

"Well, then tell me where else it goes! We can't put it there or the whole thing will fall."

"What are you guys doing?" Manda asked.

Ry turned to her, with a long stick in her hand. "Well, there was this glowing snowman in the crates that Kass and I decided to set up along with the snowglobe and penguins. But we don't know where this piece goes."

"We do. It goes on the back," Kass said.

"It'll fall if we put it there, though."

Fish held out her hand and Ry handed the stick to her. Fish looked at each end before stepping closer to the snowman. She looked for any opening that matched. "You are both wrong. This doesn't even go to this guy." She walked closer to the penguin on the surfboard. Placing it underneath, she said, "It goes here."

Kass and Ry looked sheepishly at each other.

"My bad. Sorry, Kass," Ry said.

Manda shook her head. "Now that that's done, there is one more thing we can put out. But we will have to get on the roof."

"Not it," came from Kass and Fish.

"Come on Ry, we can climb up there and they can hand us the parts."

Meanwhile, inside, Ma finished wrapping the staircase banister in lighted holly. She plugged it into the socket out of the way. The light glowed brilliantly red. "So, pretty."

"It is really pretty!" agreed B. She climbed off the stool she had been using to hang up the mistletoe.

"You really think that's wise?" laughed Ma.

B shrugged but smiled. "It's tradition. Besides, we don't have to kiss each other. We can just hug."

Lissa stuck her head into the hallway. "I personally want to see Kass get stuck with Manda."

The three girls laughed loudly. Lissa went back into the living room while the others followed.

"Wow, Lissa! It looks so pretty!" Ma exclaimed. "I think we are gonna win this competition!"

The room was adorned in lights and flameless candles. Fake snow-covered holly surrounded the fireplace mantel. There were several nutcrackers adorning the shelves. She had lit a fire so it crackled and sent off the scent of oak throughout the room.

"Thanks! I added the nutcrackers for Ry. Maybe sway her a little bit," Lissa said.

Ma put her finger to her nose. "Good thinking. Should we go check out the village that B and I did in the dining room?"

The girls walked back across the hall. The shelves and cabinets were now covered in fluffy fake snow, and the scene they made looked amazing. There were people going to and fro with packages and smiling and waving at each other. There was a park scene with people ice skating and kids having a snowball fight.

"This looks amazing!" exclaimed Lissa. "No way we are going to lose."

The girls agreed and went to put on their coats and shoes to go check on the others outside. They walked off the porch to find Manda and Ry climbing down from the roof. They moved the boxes and ladder back into the shed.

"You guys come to cry when we win?" Fish said.

"No, more to gloat," laughed Ma.

Manda grabbed the plug and stood next to the outlet. "Well, prepare to be amazed!" She plugged it in and the whole yard and porch lit up brightly. The Squad gasped collectively.

"Well, there's no way Santa will miss us now," Lissa said.

Fish, Ry, Manda, and Kass high fived each other. They knew they did good. The lit-up sleigh and reindeer on the roof was the icing on the cake. They stood for a few more minutes before heading inside. The inside looked just as amazing as it did outside. They couldn't figure out a clear winner, so they all drew straws to see who was cooking breakfast.

The group then decided to set up the tree and have snacks for dinner while they trimmed it. Manda and Kass started making the snacks as the others brought in the tree. Lissa made sure there was plenty of water in the base as Fish cut off a few dead branches. Ry helped Manda and Kass bring in the platters of food. The rest of the evening they hung lights and ornaments on the tree. When the tree was done, they all helped clean up and decided it was about time to get ready for bed. B had already been dozing off on a chair in the corner.

The next morning, Manda headed downstairs to make sure Kass and Fish had what they needed for breakfast. While she pulled out the biscuits, a knock came at the door. She walked to it. After looking in the peephole and seeing no one, Manda opened the door slowly. There was no one in sight and the snow on the steps seemed untouched. She stepped out and saw that in the night snow had fallen hard and their cars were now snowed in.

"That's weird," she said to herself.

"What's weird?" asked Kass, making Manda jump.

"Dude!" Manda said, clutching her chest. "You can't sneak up on me like that."

Kass smirked. "My bad. Now, what's weird?"

"There was a knock on the door but no one is here and the snow hasn't been messed with. Also, it doesn't look like we are going to town today."

Manda turned back toward the open door. There was another gift basket sitting to the side of the door. Picking up the note, Manda read:

"Good morning! We noticed the snow was picking up last night and knew you would be snowed in. Your trip into town would be changed, so we wanted to make sure you had some extra food and items you would need while you were snowed in. We hope you are all having a good time.

Merry Christmas!

The Pelznickels

P.S. The decorations look amazing!"

Manda looked at the basket and found a big ham, vegetables and other things. Kass helped her pick it up and take it inside to the kitchen.

"Well, what are we gonna do now?" Kass asked.

Fish walked into the kitchen. "What do you mean?"

"Well, apparently it snowed a lot last night and now we're snowed in." Manda answered. "We were supposed to go into town today."

The girls set to making breakfast as they threw out ideas. When everyone had made it down to the dining room, Manda told everyone what was happening.

"So, I'm not sure what to do now, but we've been snowed in," Manda said. "So, we won't be able to go into town today. Thankfully the owners dropped off the food we need to make dinner for tomorrow."

"You mean, they drove up here, in the heavy snow to drop off food?" asked Ma.

"I have no clue," Manda said, shrugging. "None of the snow looked like it had been disturbed, but how else would they have gotten it up here?"

"And another thing, how did they know what we were planning on cooking? Or that we hadn't bought any of it yet? These owners sound suspicious," Ry piped up.

Everyone started nodding in agreement except Manda. "I mean, when we met, they asked if we had plans and we may have discussed a few of them. They seem like really nice people if I'm honest."

"But how would they just know exactly what we needed? And how did they bring it all to us? Sounds like they have cameras or something," Fish added.

"The Pelznickels don't seem like the type to spy on us though. He even had trouble with his phone when he went to find the code to send me for the door."

B stirred. "What were their names?"

Manda frowned. "Chris and Janet Pelznickel."

"Oh, my goodness," B laughed. "Guys, they aren't suspicious. They are Mr. and Mrs. Clause."

Ry put her hand on B's forehead. "Do you have a fever? Santa isn't real."

"So says you. But Pelznickel was a name given to Santa in some cultures. I'm telling you, they know because they are magical." B folded her arms across her chest. She was standing her ground and not relenting.

"Well, whether or not they are Santa and Mrs. Clause, we still don't know what to do today," Ma interjected.

"It seems that plans we make always end up changing," laughed Kass.

Fish smiled. "They don't call us the Chaos Squad for nothing. I say we check the shed again. Maybe they have some things in there."

They finished breakfast and headed back out to the shed. Manda picked up some snow and balled it. She then threw it at Kass who was in front of her. Kass turned and picked up her own ball of snow. She threw it at Manda who easily dodged it. It hit B right in the face. Before they even made it to the door, an epic snowball fight broke out. Manda, B, and Ma against Fish, Ry, Kass, and Lissa. The girls used all the freshly fallen snow to make a snow wall to hide behind and then made stockpiles of snowballs. B and Ma started lobbing them at the others. A few found their targets with grunts followed by laughter.

"Eat my snow!" yelled Ry as she threw a snowball at Manda. It hit her in the chest and she went down.

B ran to her and picked up her head. "No! Manda! You can't go! We need you!"

Trying to look as if she were dying, Manda reached up to B's red cheeks. "B, you and Ma will have to go on without me."

Kass laughed. "You guys are so dramatic."

"And you are unarmed," came Ma's voice as a snowball smacked Kass in the side.

The group gathered together as they laughed loudly. Their impromptu snowball fight had been fun. But they were a little tired. They continued to the shed. They all found something to sit on to catch their breath. Fish pointed out a couple sleds in the back of the shed. She and Ry grabbed them. They were large enough that two people could fit at a time. They decided to use them to race each other down the hill. Kass, Ma, and Lissa told them they were gonna sit this one out because they wanted to build a snowman.

Manda and Ry chose one sled, and B and Fish took the other. They placed them at the top of the hill and climbed on. Fish counted them down and they let loose. They all laughed as they raced down the hill faster and faster. They hit the bottom and the sleds skidded to a halt.

"I think we won!" cried B.

"You just got lucky," said Ry. "Let's go again."

The girls trudged back up the hill with their sleds in tow. Going back up took longer than getting down. By the time they reached the top, the snowman the others were making had taken shape. Manda and Ry set their sled back down on the starting point.

"Manda, hey let me sit in the back this time. My legs are longer and might give us some extra umph," Ry whispered.

Nodding, Manda moved to sit at the front. She grabbed the rope and then settled her arm over Ry's feet to help keep her seated. Fish counted off again and Manda yanked the rope hard while Ry pushed off. Their sled took off like a rocket. Manda could tell they were going faster than Fish and B, but something was off. Before she could react, the sled slipped sideways. Manda let go of Ry's feet and watched her slide off the side. With no other way to stop herself, Manda pulled on the rope to try and correct herself. The sled flipped over and after careening about fifty more feet, it along with Manda came to a halt.

"Manda!" yelled Fish. She, B, and Ry ran over to her.

"I'm ok, for the most part." answered Manda as she sat up. "My hand is still caught in the rope though."

Ry knelt as soon as she got close enough and took Manda's hand. She carefully untangled the rope. Manda winced and sucked in her breath as it came loose.

"You have a pretty deep gash from the rope," said Ry. She took off her scarf and wrapped up Manda's hand. "There's a first aid kit back at the cabin. We need to get this cleaned up and bandaged."

Fish and B helped Manda stand. B looked scared and Fish was breathing hard from running. "Guys," Manda said, smiling at them. "I'm fine. It's just a little cut. Don't worry."

"Oh, I'm not worried." Manda wasn't sure who Fish was trying to convince, Manda or herself. "B and I will take the sleds back to the shed. Ry, you go ahead and take her inside."

Ry helped Manda back up the slope with B and Fish behind them. "I'm sorry, Manda. I was just trying to beat them."

"Accidents happen, Ry. And really, I'll be fine. It wasn't your fault at all."

They finally reached the top and Kass noticed them first. "What's going on guys? Done racing already?"

"There was a bit of a mishap. The sled went off course and my hand got caught in the rope. Ry is gonna help me clean it up, but it's best if you keep Ma over there," Manda said.

Lissa came running to them and followed Manda and Ry into the kitchen. Ry grabbed the kit and Lissa started undoing the scarf. Ry poured a little peroxide on a towel and pressed it into her hand. After she and Lissa were satisfied it was clean enough, Lissa pressed a folded gauze pad onto her hand, as Ry wrapped it up to her wrist and secured it.

"Ok, that should do it." Ry announced. "Just need to make sure you don't over use it."

"Thanks, guys," Manda said.

Lissa nodded as she helped clean up the counter. "Of course. It looks pretty bad, but as long as you keep it dry and clean, you should heal fine."

The others came in from outside. Kass and Fish came into the kitchen first. After making sure everything was cleaned up, she motioned for B and Ma to come in too.

Manda showed them Ry's handy work. "I'm all wrapped up now," she joked.

"Well, we were done with our snowman and there's plenty to do in here anyway," said Ma.

B brightened. "We could always start my favorite Icelandic tradition!"

"Oh! I'd be ok with that!" Lissa chimed in.

"Why don't we all go grab our books?" Kass suggested. "Then we can figure out who we're going to swap with."

The girls all went upstairs to their rooms and then met in the living room. Ry wrote everyone's name on a slip of paper and put them in a stocking. They all stepped forward and pulled out a slip.

"So, whoever we get is who we give our books to," B said. She opened hers. "Manda! Yay! I'm excited for you to read mine!"

Manda opened hers. "I got Ma!"

Ma ended up with Ry, while Ry had Fish. Kass gave her book to Lissa, and Fish gave hers to Kass. Everyone swapped books and opened the wrappings. They all looked at the books they were given and agreed that each one did a good job in picking something they would like.

"Before we get to reading, should we make some hot cocoa?" Lissa asked.

B stood. "I also have a drink we have in Iceland! I think you guys might like it."

"What's it called?" asked Kass. "And what's in it?"

"It's Malt og appelsín. It's made from orange soda and malt. Most people use the traditional ratio, but I'm more of a fifty-fifty."

Manda nodded. "I got everything you asked, B. It's in the kitchen. I also have eggnog and hot chocolate."

The girls all went to the kitchen to make drinks. They all grabbed a glass of B's favorite Christmas drink and then went to settle in to read. They got comfy in their chairs and listened to the crackling fire and the soft Christmas music in the background. The sun set outside and as the temperature outside dropped, but the girls inside were all cozy. Occasionally someone would laugh or sniffle at different parts of their books.

Fish's stomach growling brought the friends out of their reading states.

"I guess we should probably eat something," teased Ma.

"We still have some of the snacks from yesterday left, and we have sandwich meat and chips," Manda supplied. "So, how far along is everyone?"

Kass and Lissa both held up their books showing they had a handful of pages left. Fish was just over half way through hers, and Ma, B, and Manda had quite a bit to go.

Ry smiled sheepishly. "I may have finished already. It was really good and wasn't actually too long."

"Ooo, I'm really glad you liked it, Ry!" said Ma. "I was worried you wouldn't like it."

Ma and Ry discussed the book as they headed to the kitchen for food. They all grabbed plates and started munching on different leftovers and sandwiches. They ate around the counter in the kitchen, laughing and talking about the fun they have had so far.

They cleaned up soon after, and then decided to head to bed. Manda had to get up early to get the ham in the oven and start the other prep. Lissa said she would help so that Manda didn't get her hand dirty or wet.

"I wish we could have gone into town though. That way we could put gifts under the tree," Manda said, a little dejectedly.

"Honestly, this time together is gift enough for me. It has been amazing to be able to spend Christmas together. Don't feel bad about it," Lissa said, patting Manda's shoulder.

Manda nodded and hugged her friend before going to sleep. It had been a long day and she was exhausted.

Manda had a weird dream of Santa dropping off the gift baskets with food, and her trying to run after the reindeer to catch them. She was woken hours later by excited voices.

"Manda! Lissa! Get up! B was right!"

Manda wiped the sleep from her eyes and stood up. She followed Lissa down the stairs and into the living room. Her jaw dropped when she entered.

Underneath the tree were several brightly colored boxes with bows. Manda checked a couple tags and saw that they were for them. She looked at the mantel and saw all seven stockings filled to the brim.

"What in the world?" she whispered more to herself.

"Here," said B. She passed a card over to Manda as her smile lit-up her entire face. "There was a card left for you."

Manda opened it and saw the now familiar handwriting of the Pelznickels:

"Manda,

We wanted to thank you for staying at the Christmas Cabin.

The Mrs and I know that Christmas is a magical time to spend with your loved ones. As a token of our appreciation, the gifts under the tree are for you and the rest of the Chaos Squad. We sincerely hope your time here has been fun, blessed, and full of love. Have the Merriest of Christmasses!

Sincerely,

The Pelznickels

P.S. Don't stop believing in the magic of Christmas! There are miracles all around, if you look for them."

Manda stood in disbelief as the rest of her friends came downstairs. She saw the joy in each one of their faces as they started opening their gifts. They all laughed and giggled, throwing the paper and ribbon at each other. She joined in, and soon her cheeks hurt from laughing so much.

Today would be one of the best days of her life. The fact that they were all together was the only important thing. She would always believe in Santa, and she would never forget the year that her Christmas had been filled with Chaos.

The Christmas That Almost Wasn't

By: C.J. Peterson

Author C. J. Peterson

C.J. Peterson is a multi-award-winning, multi-genre published author since 2012. She is also a podcaster, blogger, and publisher who knows how to relate well to folks of all ages.

She has multiple series out: ***Grace Restored Series***, ***The Holy Flame Trilogy***, and the ***Divine Legacy Series*** for young adults and adults, where the characters crossover storylines. It's an edge of your seat journey, that will have you holding onto the pages for dear life! The stand-alone book, ***Strength From Within***, is also a part of this series, along with the Christmas novella: ***Christmas A.N.G.E.L.s***!

The Sands of Time Trilogy is an exciting Christian Fiction SciFi series! This series follows a group of teens with abilities as they go through the US to rescue their siblings. The challenger is their sadistic creator who has the money & power to win at any cost.

She also just released a time travel book with a twist! Tripp and Tori travel back in time to fix their family line. In doing so, will they make so many changes that they cease to exist? Find out in *Chain Reaction!*

https://cjpetersonwrites.com

"While the stories are fiction, the journey is real."

C.J. has a children's book series based on the real-life *Adventures of Chief and Sarge*! She and her husband take Chief (stuffed koala) & Sarge (stuffed monkey) on real-life adventures in order to share them with your little one!

The Adventures of Chief and Sarge: Every day is an adventure with these two!

https://cjpetersonwrites.com/chief-and-sarge

The Christmas That Almost Wasn't

⌒⌒⌒

19 DEC 2026

"Tori!" Tripp jostled Tori, as she slept with her husband, Liam, in their deep east Texas home. Their children rested in their own rooms on either side of the master suite.

"Who are you? What's going on?" Liam demanded. He and Tori had been married for two years by that point. Liam rubbed his eyes and looked again.

"What?" Tori asked, sitting up. "Tripp? Tripp!" she squealed, throwing her arms around him. "I've missed you!"

"Who is that, and what is he doing in our bedroom in the middle of the night?" Liam growled. "As a matter of fact, how did you get in here?"

"I'm her great-great-great-grandson," Tripp said with a smirk.

Liam furrowed his brow. "Tori?" he asked.

"He's telling the truth," Tori said. "He's the one I traveled through time with to fix the family."

Liam gestured toward him. "He's Tripp?"

"Yes. I am," Tripp said. "Congratulations on your daughter. She's what? A year old now?"

"Yes," Tori said. "Little Elizabeth Victoria turned a year last week. And Tripp is three now."

"Elizabeth Victoria & Tripp – both good choices. You have sufficiently carried on the family names with your little ones. You've even got your nursing degree. Now, we need to make a new tradition in our family, starting in 1650."

Tori nodded, remembering the journal their relative Maggie told them about in 1922. "The Christmas that almost wasn't."

"Here are your clothes," Tripp said, handing her a bag of clothing for women from 1650 Ireland.

Liam turned on the light and looked at Tripp's clothes for the first time. "Wow! Those look authentic."

"They are," Tripp said. "I went back and got both of us a couple outfits."

"Can I come too?" Liam asked.

"No," Tripp said. "If something happens you need to be here for the babies."

"I'm a history professor. I could be of great use," Liam offered.

"Who will look after the little ones, sweetheart?" Tori asked.

Liam frowned. "Fine."

"Maybe we can take a trip when I get back," Tori suggested to his delight.

"When will you be back?" Liam asked as Tori slid out of bed and went into the bathroom to change.

"It will seem like moments to you," Tripp explained. "I will protect her and bring her back."

"You'd better or there is no time you can escape to in order to stop me from finding you," Liam threatened. "That woman has been through enough. Do *not* get her hurt!"

"I won't. I promise. I will put myself in front of her before that happens. If it helps, Maggie said we were fine. Well, the journal said we were fine. It said travelers came during Christmas to the clans and brought with them a message of hope."

"Is that all it said?" Liam asked.

"That, and that we brought Christmas to the village, and Christianity to their family. There were also pictures of both of us in the journal."

Liam whistled as he looked beyond Tripp to see Tori come out of the bathroom. "You look amazing! Good thing you are dressing warm. It's going to be cold," he pointed out. "Oh! I have something for you," he said, jumping out of bed.

"What is it?" Tori asked.

"This," he said, pulling out a bag from the back of the closet. "It's a medical bag. You don't know what will happen when you go back. You have the medical training now."

"She cannot take back anything that is not from that time," Tripp warned.

"It is, but it isn't," Liam said with a twinkle in his eyes. "Tori told me eventually you would be going back to 1650 Ireland. Since then, I have been researching medical things from that time period and area. I looked up herbal remedies from back then and stocked a bag. I also added some things you may need, Tori, at the bottom, like antibiotic ointment, but put it in an unlabeled container. No one but you will know what it is. I tore strips for bandages. I also put in some tools should you need to do any type of surgery. They are sterilized. In another container, there is alcohol for sterilizing. Those are the only things that are from this time. Everything else is from 1650...at least the plants exist there. People may not know what to use them for, but *you* do. You studied herbology in school during your nursing as an elective. Right?"

"I did," Tori agreed. "Thank you," she said and kissed him as she took the bag from him. "I don't know what I would do without you."

"I aim to never let you find out," he said, hugging her.

"Ready?" Tripp asked, typing the date, time, and location into his TORI. A TORI is a wrist device used in time travel. It stands for: Traveling, Over, Range, Indicated. It's what they used to travel through time.

Tori went to her desk and pulled her TORI out. "Still charged," she said with a smile. She handed it to Tripp to type in the information while she hugged Liam. "You, my love, I will miss!"

"Only for a few minutes on his side," Tripp pointed out.

Tori rolled her eyes. "Semantics."

Tripp chuckled. "We're going in on Thursday, December 23rd, 1650," Tripp said. "We're going to go in about three in the morning."

"You *really* need to time that better. This early morning stuff stinks," Tori complained. Tripp chuckled at her remark.

"You got this, babe," Liam said. "I'll be waiting for you right here."

"I'll be right back as far as you're concerned," she said, and they shared a kiss.

"Remember, He made everything beautiful in its time," Liam encouraged. "See you when you get back. I have the little ones."

"I love you."

"I love you, too."

With her bag on her shoulder, Tori went over to Tripp and looped her arm through his. "On three?" she asked.

"On three," he agreed. "One...two...three..."

23DEC1650

Tripp and Tori disappeared from Tori's bedroom in a shimmering cascade of light, only to reappear in a forest.

"Where are we?" Tori asked.

He handed her a peanut butter and jelly sandwich. "That's for getting you up so early. See? I'm learning," he said. Then he pulled a map out of his bag.

"Good man!"

"As for where we are? We're here." He pointed to their position on the map. "We need to go here." He pointed toward an area north of them.

"Why are we so far away?" she asked, opening her sandwich. She shoved the sandwich bag in the bottom of her bag so no one could find it.

"I wanted us to walk in. I wanted us to look like regular travelers."

"Got it. Well, let's go," she said, and they left.

When they walked into town around six that morning, the town was just starting to open. Farmers and merchants were setting up tables in the square, while other merchants opened their businesses.

As the people woke, they dumped their chamber pots, which mixed with the horrific smells of the animals. The only saving grace was the bakery scent that did its best to combat the smell of waste and hay.

Tori stumbled as her boot got caught in a mud pile that was in the street...at least she hoped it was a mud pile. "I'm okay," she mumbled.

"I thought the streets would at least have some stone by now, but I guess not," Tripp commented as they continued.

Seeing the tall castle in the background, Tori stopped and looked at it. It was considerably smaller as most castles go, but it was a castle nonetheless. It was made of stone, with stained-glass for the windows. There was one bigger tower in the middle. Tori guessed that was where the lord of the clan lived. Then, there were smaller spires on each corner, with a stone wall surrounding it.

As for the town, there was a stone entrance, but the fence surrounding the village was made of wood. The tiny houses were a mix of thatch for the roofs and stone or mud for the homes. Many of the businesses they stopped in had wood floors, and the walls were a mix of stone and wood.

"Where are the Christmas decorations?" Tori whispered to Tripp. Every once and a while, she would see holly around the door frame, and/or a candle in the window. Most of the homes and buildings did not have any evidence it was Christmas.

"You have to remember that Cromwell has outlawed Christmas," Tripp explained. "The candles are the Catholics. They light them to let other Catholics know they are doing mass. The holly is to keep spirits away for the winter solstice. Soldiers would go door-to-door arresting people who are celebrating Christmas."

"That makes no sense!"

"It was a control move. Irish love their celebrations. The English wanted them to comply, so they took away any amount of joy they could. At this point, most of the Irish lords have gone to Spain to get help, but they will not return. There are still a few around, such as the lord of this clan, Clan ó Conchobhair. The lord's name is Lord Bran, and the lady's name is Lady Genevieve. They are fair in their treatment of their people."

Tori raised an eyebrow. "Clan ó Conchobhair?"

"Distant relatives of the Conners and eventually of our family."

"So, where do we start?" Tori asked.

"How about we pour a little money into the system?" Tripp wiggled his eyebrows. "Help people have a good Christmas, even if they can't celebrate it."

"How?"

"Like this," Tripp said, going up to a cart that had various toys out for sale. He picked up a doll and handed it to Tori. "This would be great for Victoria, yeah?"

"Definitely. And, these would be great for Tripp," she said, picking up two wooden toys. Then she quietly added so only he could hear, "Of course, they will probably be in glass containers because their value will be through the roof in our time period, but they can have them."

"Consider it an investment," he said, and paid for the toys as Tori slid them into her bag. "Now to take care of that historian husband of yours."

"Meaning?"

He gestured toward the print shop. "There should be something in there we can get for him. Even if it's a small pamphlet, the age alone will have tremendous value."

They went inside, where the printer was putting a small book together. "Morning," he said with a nod.

"Good morning. Do you have any finished books we could look at and maybe purchase?" Tripp asked.

"I do, but they are probably more than you would like to pay."

"May we see them?"

"All I have are those books over there. I use them for style choices."

"Would you be willing to sell some of these to us?"

"They cost. I have to replace them if I sell them," the printer warned.

"I understand." Tripp went over and picked up a copy of *Romeo and Juliette*. He looked at Tori, whose eyes were wide. They purchased three of the books. While Tripp paid heavily for them, he knew they were worth it. They got *Romeo and Juliette*, *Macbeth*, and *A Midsummer Night's Dream*. They would be for Tripp, Tori, and Liam.

"I know these cost a lot, but they are worth it," Tori said, almost giddy.

"I know. Please contain your excitement."

"But –"

"I get why you're thrilled. Calm down, though. We need to find some food and somewhere to sleep."

"We are literally walking through history."

"We *have* been walking through history," he reminded her. "This particular mission is to help these people actually experience Christmas. Not sure how we're going to do it, but we'll figure it out."

"How about –" Tori was cut off by a young boy running toward them carrying two apples, while the merchant chased after him, shouting for someone to stop him.

Tripp reached down and wrapped his arm around him, holding the squirming boy until the merchant caught up with them. Slapping the boy, the merchant said, "You are going to the law, laddie!"

"Sir," Tori spoke up, "may we pay for his apples...and a little extra for your trouble? Would that satisfy your sense of justice?"

The merchant looked at each of them. "Is 'e yours?"

"No, sir. Just trying to help. He looks like he could use some nourishment," Tripp said. The merchant nodded, and headed back to his stand closely followed by Tripp, Tori, and the young boy, who was now resigned to his fate.

When they arrived, Tori bought six apples, but paid twice as much. She handed the boy four of the apples. "Please do not steal again. The next person may not be so kind as this gentleman."

"I don' need yer help!" the boy said. He grabbed the apples disappeared.

"You *will* face the law next time!" the merchant yelled after him, shaking his fist. Then to Tori and Tripp, he added, "Ungrateful little lout! 'e'll get 'is next time! The law will get 'im!"

"Thank you for your kindness today," Tori said, and they left the stand.

"He's right. We probably didn't do him any favors," Tripp pointed out.

"But for today he will have food in his belly and will not be rotting away in some disgusting jail cell." When Tripp shook his head, Tori added, "Consider it a Christmas present."

"Noted. Let's get some food."

"There are no restaurants. The soonest we can sit down to eat something is when the tavern or pub opens," Tori reminded him. "What if we snack on fruit and shop until they do?"

"We can look around," Tripp agreed. "We'll need to check into an inn soon so it doesn't fill up."

For the morning, they enjoyed looking into the various stores and shops, along with just exploring the town. It was not overly huge, but the historical aspect of things fascinated both of them.

After checking into the inn around noon, they headed over to the tavern to get something to eat. Tori sat outside while Tripp went inside. He returned with a pint of ale for each of them, along with some bread and herring.

"Well, it's food," Tori said, tearing off a piece of bread. "Not too sure about the ale."

"Technically, that's all you need. It has nutritional value," Tripp defended his choices. "Besides, you don't want to know the other options."

"Probably not."

They got multiple looks from people along the street, but they ignored them.

After lunch, they returned to the inn.

"Master Tripp and Lady Tori, I have splendid news!" the innkeeper said as they walked in.

They stopped at the counter. Tripp leaned his crossed arms on it, as he asked, "What has you in such a good mood?"

"Tonight, Lord Bran and Lady Genevieve open their castle to the village for a celebration of the winter solstice. Being that you are guests of the inn, you are invited as well!"

"Wonderful!" Tripp grinned. Turning to Tori, he asked, "Did you hear that, Tori? We're going to the castle tonight!" He turned back to the innkeeper, and asked. "What time do we depart?"

"Just after dark. If you come down here, I will lead you and the other guests over to the castle. There will be a play, along with singing, stories, and food fit for a king! He does it every year. Truth be told, he feeds us from the hidden stores."

"Hidden stores?" Tripp asked.

"Yes. We must hide some of our stores from the soldiers or they will take everything. The farmers and merchants are charged with giving the castle ten percent of their wares. The castle sets aside five percent for the soldiers to see, and five percent is completely hidden. Only the lord and lady know its location."

"Fair enough. Sounds wise," Tripp said. "We shall come down when it gets close to dark. What shall we wear?"

"It is a celebration! Wear your finest!" he exclaimed.

"Thank you, my good man. We will return when it is closer," Tripp said, and they went up to their room.

The room had wood floors, one window, two twin beds, and a table. On the table was a pitcher, along with a bowl to wash their hands and faces.

After they were settled, Tripp disappeared from the room, returning several minutes later with a nice outfit for him, and a nice dress for Tori to change into for the evening.

When he held them up, Tori nodded in approval. "Very nice! God bless time travel!"

The night brought a lot of anxiety, along with curiosity for Tori. As they walked through the archway into the courtyard, she could not believe her eyes. Going back in time so far had brought amazing sights, but *this* was on another level.

As they walked through the halls, she lightly ran her fingers over the stone, knowing she was touching a piece of history that may or may not exist in her time. If the castle stood in her time, it would be a shell at best.

However, in this day, the castle was spectacular. She could not imagine the man hours it took to build this castle from stone and wood. There were chandeliers hanging from the ceiling with candles for light. In the great hall, there were tables lined on one side of the hall and the benches for those tables were set up in the other side for people to watch the play in a bit. There were small holly wreaths around the candle holders and the larger candles to catch the wax.

Tori admired the ivy and holly decorations around the doorways and along the tables. There were large candles as centerpieces, alternated with candle holders with tapestry candles. She saw the holly lining the balcony area, with white bows every five feet.

This was more what she imagined Christmas in 1650 to look like. Everyone was in good spirits as they filled the hall. There was plenty of laughter and joy as people greeted others. Several even introduced themselves to Tripp and Tori.

"Please, sit by me so I can explain the play," the innkeeper offered.

"Thank you," Tripp said, as he sat beside the innkeeper. Tori sat on the other side of Tripp. "And your name again, kind sir?"

"Cullen," he said.

"Thank you, Cullen. I would think calling you by your familiar would be kinder than just sir."

"I appreciate it," he said and nodded in respect.

As the play started, it took a few moments for everyone to settle and watch. Cullen explained what went on in a hushed whisper so only Tripp and Tori could hear.

"In this story, a young lady was betrothed to marry a man she was not in love with. She tried desperately to get her parents to understand, but the young man was a lord and would improve her standing, so they were firm."

"Glad I was born when I was," Tori said quietly to Tripp.

"Agreed," he said just as quietly.

"So, when the young man she was in love with found out about the arranged marriage, the young couple took off in the night and got married," Cullen continued.

"Sounds like something I would have done," Tori whispered to Tripp, who stifled his laugh.

"When the parents of the young couple found out, they contacted the lord's parents to pay so they would not go after the young couple. There was a contingency made where the young couple had to combine their surnames. You see, they were from rival families."

"They were from rival families?" Tori asked Cullen. When he nodded, she asked, "Yet, they would allow them to stay together?"

"What God has joined together, no man can tear asunder," Cullen said.

"I see." Tori nodded. "Thank you. Please continue."

"So, after paying the debt so the young couple could stay together, the families thought their troubles were over. However, the young lord was furious. As far as he was concerned, the young lady was his."

Tori rolled her eyes. "Of course, he did."

"With respect," Cullen said, "she *was* his. The young man stole what was to be his bride."

"I see," Tori said, and tightened her lips together to remind her to watch her words.

"So, a few weeks after everything was settled, the lord killed the young man who took his bride. What he did not know was the young lady was pregnant with her first husband's child. He did not care. He still married her."

"Why did she marry him?" Tori asked. "He killed her husband."

"He saved her," Cullen explained.

"He *killed* her husband. How is that saving her?"

"She was now a widow and pregnant. She needed a husband."

Tori felt her face flush in anger. She tightened her fists to her side, as she struggled to control her tongue.

"He gave her and her son status. He saved her from being a destitute widow with a child," Cullen explained. Everyone clapped at the final scene of the couple getting married. "See? Everyone lived happily ever after."

"Except the husband," Tori let slip out.

"The young couple created the mess, but the lord cleaned it up," Cullen said.

"I just...okay," Tori said, taking deep breaths. "I applaud the actors. Very well done."

"They will appreciate that."

After the play, as people moved the benches over to the tables, and the servers brought out the food, the head of each family went before Lord Bran and Lady Genevieve to be introduced.

When it was time for those from the inn to be introduced, Cullen stayed where he was to introduce them to the lord and lady. "Lord Bran, Lady Genevieve, this is Master Tripp and Lady Tori."

Tripp and Tori bowed before the pair as they sat at the head table.

"Welcome. What brings you here?" Lord Bran asked.

"We are travelers from The Colonies," Tripp said. "Our family line originated from this clan and we wished to know more."

"Family line? Are you two not married?" Lord Bran asked.

"No, m'lord," Tripp said. "Lady Tori is my sister. We lost our parents in The Colonies, and came here to explore our roots. We wanted to learn the traditions of our family and our history, so we can pass it down to the next generation."

"Admirable," Lord Bran remarked. "I look forward to speaking with you again."

"Thank you, kind sir," Tripp said, as he and Tori bowed again.

They headed over to their spot at the tables, and sat down. For an appetizer, they served a prawn cocktail. This was followed by a dinner of spiced beef, mashed potatoes, stuffing, raw carrots, peas, and raw broccoli. Then for dessert, a plum pudding, and enough ale to make the entire town drunk!

During dinner, there were stories and laughter, singing and joyful hearts. While Tripp and Tori were not a part of this clan, this night, everyone was a part of Clan ó Conchobhair.

A few hours into eating, one of the lord's servants came to Tripp and Tori, and told them that the lord and lady would like to meet with them in their sitting room. So, they got up from the table and followed the guards through the halls.

Tori thought castles were lit with torches or candles all night, but the only light in this castle at night were the lanterns being carried by the two guards in front of Tripp and Tori.

When they arrived, a guard opened the door and allowed them to enter. He handed Tripp his lantern to see. There was already a fire in the fireplace, and several lanterns lit throughout the room, making it fairly bright.

Once settled, the guard closed the door behind him, leaving Tripp and Tori with Lord Bran and Lady Genevieve alone in the room.

"Welcome," Lord Bran started. "I know it took some time to arrive to our shores. Would you mind sharing your adventure with us this evening?"

"Certainly," Tripp said. "Our parents were among those who went to Massachusetts Bay Colony when Tori and I were younger. Our father was a blacksmith and our mother was a seamstress. They did fairly well for themselves. Unfortunately, our mother died of consumption about a year ago, and our father could not handle it and took his own life."

Both Lord Bran and Lady Genevieve gasped. "I'm so sorry," Lady Genevieve said. "That is horrible!"

"It was at that point we decided to come back to where our family started in Ireland, and with this clan. We are connected many years back. When we left for Massachusetts Bay, we left from England. Tori and I wanted to learn the traditions of our true family. We wanted to experience Christmas with our clan. However, we only see what looks like Christmas here in the great hall."

"Yes. Unfortunately, Christmas is not allowed at this time, much to our sorrow," Lord Bran explained.

"Thanks to that bloody fool Cromwell!" Lady Genevieve grumbled.

"Please forgive Lady Genevieve," Lord Bran said. "She is wise, but also outspoken."

"Kind of like someone else I know," Tripp said, eyeing Tori. Then, looking back to Lady Genevieve, he added, "A lady stating her opinion is welcome. I would rather know what's going through her mind, then find out later when she is upset with me."

Lady Genevieve smiled in delight.

"Cromwell strongly discourages the actual celebration of Christmas," Lord Bran explained. Lady Genevieve huffed. "More like he sends his soldiers to arrest anyone who celebrates it."

"He states that we should utilize this time for a time of remembrance. A time of solemn humiliation to remember our sins and the sins of our forefathers who, as he puts it, *have turned this feast, pretending the memory of Christ, into an extreme forgetfulness of Him, by giving liberty to carnal and sensual delights.* I call it a celebration. I call his description bollocks."

"Bran!" Genevieve exclaimed.

"I apologize for my bluntness, but I want my people to celebrate. I want to see more of what we saw tonight, but we won't until Cromwell is gone."

"What if...what if we could bring Christmas to your kin this year?" Tripp offered.

"What do you mean?" Lord Bran asked.

"How do you normally celebrate?" Tripp asked.

"We could provide a token to each family?" Lady Genevieve suggested.

"If you have extra money, we could buy toys for the kids all during tomorrow," Tori said. "We'll tell them we're taking them back to The Colonies with us."

"Brilliant! We could also give a small amount of food and a

few coins per family," Lord Bran said, rubbing his chin. "We have it in the secret stores."

Lady Genevieve clapped her hands in delight. "The families will be thrilled!"

"This would make you happy as well?" Lord Bran asked Lady Genevieve.

"Very much so."

Turning to Tripp, he asked, "How will you achieve this? The soldiers will stop you. If they find out what you are doing, you will be arrested. Why would you risk this?"

"Seeing the joy on the faces of those tonight, brought joy to my heart," Tripp explained. "I cannot imagine what it's like for a parent to not see that joy on Christmas morning. I have a young lady I am courting, her name is Petra, but we do not have little ones as of yet."

"Of course not. You are not yet married," Lord Bran said. "And you?" he asked Tori.

"I am married with two children. My husband has allotted me this time to travel to learn the traditions of our family."

"He is braver than I," Lord Bran said with a chuckle. "Our young ones are married with young ones of their own. I do not know that I would be so courageous as to allow Lady Genevieve to leave them in my care for an extended period of time without another to look after them. They may not be the same when she returned."

Everyone giggled.

"Now," Lord Bran looked pointedly at Tripp and Tori, "if we provide the money for the toys, and you return to the castle tomorrow for small bags of food and a few coins for each family, you promise to deliver these by Christmas morning?"

"We do," Tripp assured him.

"We will," Tori agreed.

Getting up from his chair, Lord Bran went over to his desk. He pulled out a leather pouch and shook it. Then he walked back to the group, handed Tripp the pouch, and retook his seat. "The matter is settled. Thank you for this. Please return after you have finished shopping for the children."

Lady Genevieve got up and retrieved a leather-bound journal. She handed it to Tori before returning to her seat. "This is the list of the families in the clan and their children. It also has a map. With this, you can determine how much to leave at which house."

"Thank you. We will return this Christmas morning," Tori promised.

"Agreed," Lord Bran said with a smile.

Together, they chatted for a few more hours. Tori's mind was a bit blown that she was speaking with her ancestors from 1650. She would journal about this experience as soon as she returned to her time period so she could treasure the memory forever.

24DEC1650

The next morning, Tripp and Tori set to work. They made sure to also purchase a few burlap bags to contain the toys. When one was full, they would take it back to the inn. As per their word, they told the villagers the toys were going to the children in The Colonies when they returned.

In order to pull this off, they enlisted the help of Cullen, the innkeeper, to keep their secret in helping to gather the presents and keep an eye out for the soldiers.

Around two that afternoon, Tripp and Tori returned to the castle as requested by Lord Bran and Lady Genevieve.

Once ushered to the sitting room, they were momentarily joined by Lord Bran and Lady Genevieve, who took seats across from them. "Word has spread of your purchases," Lord Bran said with a smile. "Seems you are already spreading Christmas cheer by making the merchants happy."

"Yes. We have also purchased bread to leave for the families," Tripp explained. "The baker should finish the order soon."

Lord Bran pulled a bag from behind his chair and handed it to him. When Tripp took it, he was not expecting it to weigh so much. The coins jingled as Tripp took possession of the bag, almost dropping it.

"That coin is for the families, along with a small bag of rice for each," Lord Bran explained.

"How do you intend on doing this all in one night?" Lady Genevieve asked.

"That is our secret. But rest assured, it will be done," Tripp said.

Lord Bran sat back in his seat, resting his hands over his stomach. "I hate to get excited and not have it happen."

"It *will* happen," Tripp said firmly. "Trust us."

"We are putting much faith in you, complete strangers to us," Lady Genevieve pointed out. "However, there is something familiar...endearing about the pair of you that propels us to trust you."

"We will not betray that trust. Your kin will wake up to special gifts from you," Tripp assured them.

"Be safe, and go with God," Lord Bran said, and they headed back to the inn to sort through everything.

For the rest of the afternoon, they sorted piles for each family, separating the toys, bread, coins, and rice. Once everything was sorted, they placed them in individual bags. The bags were tied closed, with pieces of parchment paper and the family name on them. Once finished, they placed them back in the burlap bags for that night.

Around seven that night, Tori and Tripp jumped when someone pounded on their door. "Quick! Put these on the other side of your bed," Tripp said. After Tori put the bags on the other side of the bed, Tripp opened the door.

"You must hurry!" Cullen said, panic written all over his body. "The soldiers have entered the town. They are going door to door. You must grab the bags and follow me immediately!" Tripp, Tori, and Cullen all grabbed two sacks each and headed down to the bottom floor. In Cullen's room, he already had a table moved, along with a rug, which showed a trap door leading to a hidden room. Tripp and Tori climbed in. Once they were down there, Cullen passed the bags down to them.

"Please be quiet. The soldiers are not to know you are here," Cullen warned. When Tripp and Tori nodded, he closed the trap door. Then he covered the door with a rug and a leg of the table. Several minutes later, Tori jumped when she heard the door fly open to the inn. It was so loud she was certain the door was torn off. She hugged the sack nearest to her while she held her breath.

Tripp pulled the sleeve on his wrist up to show his TORI set to return to her time, so Tori set hers to match. If they needed to, they would hit the button to return to their time.

"Where are they?" a soldier demanded.

"My guests are either in their room or out," Cullen said innocently.

"We are looking for the two called Lord Tripp and Lady Tori. We understand they did a lot of purchasing."

"They did," Cullen acknowledged. "However, they have since left for the docks. Possibly returning to The Colonies. I know they purchased a lot of toys to take back with them."

"Toys and baked goods?" the soldier questioned. "Are they planning on feeding the entire ship?"

"I do not know their plans. I only run this inn."

"You are worthless!" the soldier said, and shoved Cullen aside as the soldiers tore through the inn.

While the soldiers searched the inn, Tori hugged the sack tighter. The dust was coming through the floorboards. Tori thought sure they could hear her heart pounding in her chest.

Tripp reached over and held her hand in support. She finally let out the breath of air she was holding when they left the room. However, she did not move a muscle until they finally left the inn about thirty minutes later.

Cullen waited for another four hours before he finally opened the door. "Many apologies. I had to wait until I knew for sure the soldiers had cleared the village and would not return tonight. I hope you still have time to do your mission."

"We do," Tripp assured him, as he helped him out of the hole. Tripp grabbed the bags that Tori handed up to him before he helped her out.

"This is a lot. Are you sure you can do this?" Cullen asked, looking at all the sacks.

"We will."

"I pray you are correct. Lord Bran and Lady Genevieve do not normally put this much trust in people. They are good folk, but since his father left for Spain, he has been on edge, expecting betrayal to come from one direction or another," Cullen explained, as they headed upstairs each carrying two sacks.

"We will complete the task," Tori assured him. "This is just as important to us as it is to them."

"Why?"

"Because we have had so much hurt in our lives, seeing the joy in everyone last night is something we want to experience again," Tori said. "Life is rough all around. We heard the stories of how our ancestors used to celebrate life. We want to experience that again. We want to bring that joy to others, starting in this little corner of the world."

"I understand. I pray you will accomplish just that," he said, setting his sacks on the ground in their room. "Please be careful. There is no telling where the soldiers are right now. They could be waiting outside of town or hiding in the alleys. They were looking specifically for you in this inn. They know something is amiss."

"We understand. Thank you," Tripp said. "Please do not disturb us until morning."

"Agreed," Cullen said, and then headed back downstairs, as Tripp locked the door behind him.

Once the door was secured, Tripp turned to Tori and said, "It's time to start our mission."

"How are we going to do this?"

Tripp held up his wrist, showing his TORI. With a sly smile, he said, "We're going to do it with a little help from technology."

"Fair enough. Commence Operation Clan Christmas," Tori said with a grin. She put one of the sacks over her shoulder and added, "I feel like Santa Clause."

"More like Santa's helper. Let's go."

25DEC1650

Tripp and Tori took turns using their TORIs so neither TORI drained completely. That way, if they had to escape, they would still have the power to travel hundreds of years back to the future.

They finally finished around four that morning, and collapsed in their beds out of pure exhaustion. They successfully saved the Christmas that almost wasn't. How it played out in the morning, they would have to wait and see. At this point, their TORIs were still charged enough to get them back home.

Around ten that morning, Tori woke with a start from someone pounding on their door. Tripp stumbled out of his bed over to the door, while Tori covered her head with a pillow.

"A thousand pardons, m'lord and m'lady, but Lord Bran and Lady Genevieve request your presence at the castle immediately," Cullen explained.

"Thank you. We will leave momentarily."

Cullen bowed and headed back downstairs, while Tripp locked the door. "Tori, we've been summoned. I suggest we pack first. We may need to make a quick exit."

"Got it," she groaned. "I'm tired."

"I get it, but when the Lord and Lady of the clan call, you jump or you could find yourself in jail."

"Agreed."

When they arrived to the sitting room, Lord Bran and Lady Genevieve were already waiting for them, and there was a man sitting in the corner looking at them.

"Please disregard him. He will be drawing," Lord Bran said. "Please, have a seat." He gestured toward the two seats across from him and Lady Genevieve.

"We have heard the people rejoicing this morning," Lady Genevieve explained. "They are saying it is a Christmas miracle. How did you accomplish this? We are aware of how late the soldiers were here last night. How is this possible?"

"We are going to share something with you," Tripp said. "You trusted us to get the job done, so we are going to trust you with this secret."

"What secret?" Lord Bran asked.

"We are travelers," Tripp started.

"We are aware. You traveled from The Colonies."

"While it is true we traveled from what you call The Colonies, we do not call it that anymore. In our time, it is referred to as the United States of America. The world is open to anyone in our time."

"You mean by ships?" Lord Bran asked.

"No. We mean by planes, ships, cars, and trains, there are various forms of transportation."

Lord Bran shook his head. "I do not understand."

"We are not from this time. Tori is from 2026, and I am from the year 2187."

"How is this possible?"

"We traveled back in time to help you celebrate Christmas. It was important to us. We also came back with a message for you about Jesus Christ."

"We know of Jesus Christ."

"But, do you *know* Him?" Tripp challenged. "Do you have a relationship with Him? Just as we spoke about passing the family traditions down to the next generation, this is a divine legacy that can be passed to each generation as well. It's the legacy of a relationship with a living God. It is a relationship with Jesus Christ, who walks with us daily. It is a relationship with the Holy Spirit who guides and directs our steps. Do you have a Bible?"

"Yes. The family Bible is over there." Lord Bran gestured toward a giant Bible on a stand.

They went over, and Tripp showed them the following sections: Luke 1:26-38; Luke 2:1- 21; Matthew 2:1-12; Matthew 27; and then Luke 24. Afterward, they returned to their chairs.

"This Jesus, you know Him?" Lord Bran asked.

"Yes. We both do," Tripp said.

"I did not initially know Him," Tori explained. "As we traveled through time, I learned more about Him. He was the same Jesus in 1813, as He was in 1922, as He was in 1987, as He was in 2026. He is the same in this time as well. He wants to help you and love you. He wants a relationship with you, but you have to make the first step. You have to pray and ask Him to lead you. You have to study His Word and learn to apply it to your life. People are people at their core, no matter when they're born. That Bible provides you with what you need to survive this life and beyond."

"Thank you. We will consider these words," Lord Bran said. "We are grateful for your appearance this year for Christmas. We cannot thank you enough for bringing joy to the hearts of our kin."

"Jesus is the only way to keep that joy permanently in your hearts and their hearts," Tripp said. "To lead with a strong heart, your heart must be just as strong."

"It seems our conversation needs to make a turn toward this Jesus Christ. Please, tell me more?" Lord Bran asked.

After their meeting, Tripp and Tori left the castle. Tori kept a continuous watch over her shoulder. "I don't feel comfortable in staying anymore. While I respect them, and think it won't be a problem, they now know we're from the future. That is a heavy temptation for anyone."

"Agreed. Let's get back and get our stuff."

When they returned to the inn, Tripp put a small bag of coins on the bed for Cullen. Then they gathered their bags and set their TORIs. Just as they finished, they heard multiple people on the steps.

"They're here," Tori said.

Tripp nodded. "On three. One...two...three," he said, and they simultaneously hit the buttons on their TORIs.

As the pounding on the door started, they disappeared into a shimmering cascade of light.

19DEC2026

When they reappeared, they were back in Tori and Liam's bedroom just a few minutes after they disappeared.

"Oh! Thank God you two are okay!" Liam said, jumping out

of bed. He wrapped his arms around Tori. "I'm so glad you're safe."

"Would it help if I told you I didn't even have to use the medical bag?" Tori asked.

"Yes."

"And that the timeline is still intact?"

"Yes."

"Let's make sure of that," Tripp said, pulling out the family journal from his bag.

"Is that...?" Liam's heart raced. The journal's fragility showed its age. "May I?" he asked. When Tripp handed him the journal, Liam carefully skimmed through it. He let out a low whistle. "This is amazing!"

"Our family has kept it in mint condition," Tripp said proudly.

Tori looked over Liam's shoulder. She put her hand out to stop him from flipping. "Uh, not sure how well we did in keeping the timeline intact."

"Why?" Tripp asked.

Liam read aloud, "*Lord Tripp and Lady Tori said they were travelers from the future. They did amazing things while they were here. They provided a Christmas for our clan, despite the soldier's best efforts to negate it. Each person and family received a surprise when they awoke on Christmas morning. When they came to the castle, they showed and told us of Jesus Christ. They also told us of God, The Father, and the Holy Spirit. Before they left, we gave our lives over to Christ. A lightness of our spirits occurred. They provided us a message of hope. After we sent them on their way, Genevieve and I called them back to find out more about the future. However, when the guards returned, they said when they arrived to the room, there was a beautiful light that came under the door. When it was opened, they were gone. Were they really travelers from the future, or were they messengers from God Himself? Were we visited by our future kin, or were we visited by angels? Time will tell.*"

"We are *definitely not* angels!" Tripp laughed.

"Far from it. Thank you for keeping me safe," Tori said, giving him a hug. "Until next time," he said and disappeared.

"Until next time," she agreed.

To learn more about Tripp and Tori's time traveling adventures, check out: *Chain Reaction* by C.J. Peterson. "While the stories are fiction, the journey is real."

DECK THE HALLS

BY:
VERONICA SMITH

Author Veronica Smith

Veronica Smith is a lover of all things horror. Whether she's reading, writing, or watching; that's what you will find her doing when she isn't at her day job. She treats every day as if it was Halloween and hasn't yet been fired for decorating her office as if it's a haunted house. She's been writing since 2014, when her first short story was published, and works on several projects simultaneously. She lives in Katy with her husband of over thirty years.

You can find her at:

https://viewAuthor.at/VeronicaSmith

https://godless.com/collections/godless-authors/products/veronica-smith-1 www.amazon.co.uk/-/e/B014JCZQT4

www.facebook.com/Veronica.Smith.Author

www.twitter.com/Vee_L_Smith

www.goodreads.com/author/show/862258.Veronica_Smith

Deck the Halls

ᏨᎳᎲᎩ

"Here again?"

Rosalinda looked above the gaily decorated desk to see a smiling face. Garland with red berries and gold tinsel lined the edge of the desk. There was a small Christmas tree sitting on the corner, maybe two feet tall, adorned with tiny ornaments and a star the size of quarter.

Marvin, the security guard, glanced up at the wall clock that read 11:15pm. "Why so late?"

Marvin was guarding the front doors to the small hospital where Rosalinda's husband, Joaquin, was a patient. He'd been there for over a week and looked like it would be another week more. A serious case of pneumonia in his left lung was trying to do its worst. Joaquin was feeling exceptionally down since he would still be in the hospital beyond Christmas Day.

Rosalinda chuckled. "Well, it *is* Christmas Eve. I can't leave him alone for that. I know it's late, but I have a few presents to sneak into his room while he is asleep and for a few others."

Marvin raised an eyebrow curiously. "What others?"

"I noticed there were several rooms that have patients in them, yet I never see any visitors," she replied, lifting a separate bag to

179

show Marvin the bulges. "I want to leave them some presents to know someone is thinking of them."

The smile on Marvin's face grew wider.

"That is such a sweet thing to do. I'm sure they will appreciate it," he told her. "You're like a secret Santa."

They shared a laugh and he quickly pointed to a different door, a large, flocked wreath hung on the front, miniature wrapped presents were scattered among the leaves.

"With the holiday and a much smaller crew today, they have some of the doors locked. If you go to the end of the hall and take that elevator up to the fifth floor, you can get to his room the back way. These elevators here," he motioned the other direction, "have been locked down for security."

"Okay thanks!" Rosalinda said cheerfully, and quickly placed a bright red gift box in front of Marvin. "Speaking of Santa. Haha! If I don't see you again have a Merry Christmas. Don't open it until tomorrow."

"I'll put it under *my* tree at home when I get off shift." Marvin thanked her, as he set the present next to the small tree. "You have a Merry Christmas as well."

Rosalinda walked through the doors to the elevator, her soft soles barely making a sound on the smooth tiles. The hallways just oozed Christmas. Stockings lined the walls, all with names glued to them in glitter. She assumed they were either employees or patients; or maybe both. She paused to look at a group of mini candy canes taped to a wall in the shape of a Christmas tree and fondly remembered her mother doing the same when she was little.

When the elevator doors opened, there was a ding, echoed loudly and she flinched as she stepped inside and pushed 5. The elevator hummed and vibrated as it moved upward. Even the elevator was festooned with bright green and red ribbons. The Muzak was playing *Little Drummer Boy*. The lights on the control panel dinged with each floor.

2 - ding!

3 - ding!

4 - ding!

The elevator continued to rise, and Rosalinda pushed the button for 5 again, wondering why it didn't stop on Joaquin's floor. Almost five seconds later the car finally stopped, and the doors opened. The wall directly in front of her was completely blank. Normally there would be a giant number to correspond with the floor and at least some kind of decoration or announcement.

She stepped out cautiously and peered down the hall in both directions. There was no one in sight. The lights were dim and there wasn't a sound to be heard.

"Hello?" she called out softly.

In a panic she jumped back into the elevator and set down her bags, hitting the *Close Door* button. Nothing happened. She pushed the *Emergency* button, which should have called 911, but it didn't make a sound. Frantically she pushed all the buttons.

The elevator remained open.

Tentatively, she stepped out again and walked to the right. She kept checking behind her afraid the doors would shut behind her, but they were frozen in place.

"Hello?" she called out, a little louder this time.

She decided to check inside the patient's room, although she hated to disturb them. The emptiness of the floor had her very uneasy. The first one she came to was on the right. She opened the door and found an elderly woman asleep in the bed. An IV snaked from her arm to the bag hanging above her.

"I'm sorry to bother you, but I need some help." Rosalinda whispered, stepping closer to the bed.

The woman didn't respond, just continue to breathe softly

but rhythmically. Rosalinda was getting scared now and risked the woman's ire by reaching out and shaking her gently.

Still no response.

Next to the woman's arm was the *Nurse* button. Rosalinda pushed it, hoping to hear a reply from a nurse or anyone.

But there was nothing.

Rosalinda backed out of the room and ran to the next room. A young man with his leg in a cast was deeply asleep. He also wouldn't react to her prodding, and there was no response to the emergency button. She ran into the attached bathroom and yanked on the emergency cord hanging next to the toilet. Surely that should get someone's attention.

But all was silent.

She ran out of the room, intending to go back to the elevator to try the buttons again, but when she turned around, she found a different and brighter hallway replacing the one she'd just come down. The direction she had been originally going was getting darker, as if all the lights were slowing going out, one after another, closer and closer to her. In terror, she turned and ran down the bright hallway. It turned to the left into another corridor, and she very nearly ran into a cart laden with food trays parked in front of a closed door. She gave it a wide berth and almost screamed when the door opened. An older man with a long, curly, white beard stepped out. He was quietly closing the door, rather than let it slam behind him.

"Oh hello!" he said with a cheery smile.

His blue eyes twinkled, and he smoothed his beard down with a gnarled hand.

"Where am I?" Rosalinda asked him. "The elevator brought me here, but won't take me back."

"You're exactly where you need to be," he said mysteriously.

He went to the back of the cart and began pushing it, his round belly helping push it along the way.

Santa Claus?

Rosalinda shook her head at the outrageous idea and kept pace with him.

"What do you mean?" she asked.

The white-haired attendant just whistled a cheerful Christmas song, *Jingle Bells,* if she was hearing it correctly, and stopped in front of the next room. He rolled up the sides on the cart and slid out a tray with food and drinks upon it. The plate had a domed cover to hide whatever would pass for hospital food. Joaquin wasn't a fan of the food here and begged her to sneak in a big, greasy cheeseburger. It wasn't allowed so she couldn't, but she did slip in a small bag of M&M's once.

The man looked to her and put his finger to his lips. *Shh.*

Then he disappeared into the room. Rosalinda waited for over a minute and still he never reemerged. She pushed the door open to the room, looking for him but only saw a bald man asleep in the bed. The food tray sat on the rolling table next to him. She walked around the room but couldn't find the man she had just talked to.

"Sir?" she asked, hating to disturb the patient, but he only continued to sleep, emphasizing it with a snort and a snore. It was the same as the two she'd previously tried to wake. When she stepped back out in the hallway the cart was gone.

"No!" she cried out, no longer afraid of bothering anyone. Fear overcame her worry of disturbing others.

At this point she welcomed an angry nurse coming to shush her. Or even a patient telling her to shut up. She ran down the hall, tears beginning to fall from her eyes. She came to a stop when she saw a present sitting on the floor along the wall. It was in green wrapping paper with a gold bow and a tag on it. With shaky hands she picked up the box and read the tag.

Room 510

Joaquin was in room 527, the opposite hallway from 510. She quickly set the box back down and continued down the hallway. It curved to the right, and she froze at the sight of dozens of bags, packages, and boxes, all wrapped in Christmas paper. There were tags hanging from each one. Suddenly she noticed something missing. It was odd, but she noticed there were no rooms down this hallway, it was just plain white walls that seemed to go on forever. She walked slowly, looking back and forth from wall to wall. The sizes and shapes of all the presents were different, but she did notice they all had the exact same style white tag hanging by a gold string. She bent down and could see various room numbers on them.

Room 591, Room 443, Room P322. She knew the P designated the Pediatrics floor. She picked up the P322 package and felt the shape of the lumpy package. It had to be a teddy bear.

Quickly, she set it back down in confusion. She continued to walk and realized these hallways were much longer than the building was. There was no way she was still in the hospital.

So, where was she?

She heard the clink of metal behind her and saw the jolly attendant with his cart at the end of the hall. She sprinted down the hall, hoping to catch him before he stepped into another room and disappeared. She stopped next to him, slightly out of breath and opened her mouth to ask him for help. He looked at her and winked.

"Figured it out yet?" he asked her.

"No! I don't understand?" she answered. "I'm supposed to be with my husband right now. But I can't find his room. I can't even find his floor."

"He's fine." The man soothed. "He's just sleeping. Just like all the others. It makes it easier to get my work done."

"What work?" Rosalinda asked, suddenly scared she was talking to a psycho and hoping he didn't drug everyone.

"Ho, ho, ho!" He laughed as if he read her mind. "Nothing so ominous. Quite the opposite."

He rolled up one side of the cart again and pulled out a small box. It was wrapped in colorful Christmas paper and had a white tag attached to it. He held it out to her, urging her to take it. Rosalinda accepted the gift and looked at the man. She no longer felt any malice about him, in fact, she felt joy and happiness in his presence. The feeling flowed over her. He tilted his head at the tag, encouraging her to read it.

Room 527. Joaquin's room.

She held it away as if she thought it might blow up in her face.

"Ho, ho, ho!" The man held his round belly, which jiggled as he laughed. "He'll like it. I promise."

"It's for Joaquin?" she asked him. "What is it?"

"It's a Christmas present, of course!" he replied to her then repeated his question. "Haven't you figured that out yet? It's what they all are. It's why I'm here and why you are here now."

She looked back down the hallway, lined in presents, the quantities seeming to have tripled since she began talking to him.

"You want *me* to deliver them?" she asked. "But why me?"

"Yes, of course, you," he replied, his eyes twinkling. "I was drawn to you. Your kind heart, your compassion. You brought presents for others you didn't even know for no other reason but to make them feel good. You brought a gift to Marvin downstairs. It never even entered your mind to see if he had one for you. You enjoy giving and spreading joy. You care and that makes you special. Sometimes I need help from special people. I'm spread out pretty thin; even with all the versions of me working around the world."

"Versions?" Rosalinda asked him with awe.

He put his finger next to his nose and whispered. "Santa magic." He winked and disappeared before her eyes.

In shock, she dropped Joaquin's present.

"I sure hope this wasn't breakable." She said aloud as she picked it back up. "How am I supposed to carry them all to deliver them?" She muttered, looking down the hallway.

A bump at her back had her turning around. The food cart was there, the side walls rolled up, the shelves empty. Waiting to be filled.

Rosalinda positioned herself behind the cart and began pushing. It was much lighter than she thought it would be, even while empty. She practically skipped down the hall and stopped when she reached the now mountainous piles of presents littering the hallway.

"They don't look like they will all fit but maybe with a little Christmas magic..."

Since the patient rooms were all on the third, fourth, and fifth floors she used the three shelves on the cart to sort them numerically for easier delivery. Once she had them all loaded up, she was amazed at how neatly they all fit. Even though she knew they should never have all fit.

"Santa magic," she said and chuckled.

She began wheeling the cart down the hall, unsure of what direction she was going, but knowing she would get to the place she belonged. She hummed *Here Comes Santa Claus* as she walked, and when she finished with that, she began singing *Deck the Halls*. Normally she had a horrible singing voice, she was the first to admit it, but tonight she sang like an angel.

She turned down a few more hallways, stopping to pick up a few more presents she saw scattered around. These had names on them, rather than room numbers. She recognized one of them as the nurse's name written on the board in Joaquin's room. All of them fit on the top of the cart perfectly. She turned one more corner and she was back at the elevator. She breathed a sigh of relief and laughed in amazement.

Well, why wouldn't it be there?

She pushed the cart in, and slid in next to it, picked up her original bags, and pushed the button marked 3.

She heard a loud ding as the doors opened. The wall across from her had a large 3 with Christmas decorations circling the number. Pictures obviously drawn by children were taped randomly for all to admire. Plastic candy canes hung from the ceiling. A huge stuffed snowman leaned against one wall. It had obviously been sat in based on the indentions. She could imagine children hugging it and the happiness they felt.

"Santa's helper is here!" Rosalinda called out lightly to the nurses in a singsong voice, so as not to startle them.

At first, she was surprised to find they couldn't see her. But then she remembered.

Santa magic.

She stopped in the first room on the floor, Room P301. She reached to the bottom shelf and took out the present with the matching tag. She opened the door and stepped inside. A little girl, who couldn't be more than two or three, was asleep, chest tubes snaking to the box on the floor. Her heart bled for the child and the pain she might be in. She hoped the present she brought would bring her a little pleasure. She heard a light snoring and saw a woman on the bench seat along the wall, covered in a blanket. The girl's mother. She wished she had something to leave for her as well.

Look on the cart.

She bent over and looked at the spot she'd just removed the present from. There was a tiny gift bag sitting there. As she picked it up, she watched other small presents materialize, hovering above each of the gifts for the children.

Maybe she should wish for a winning lottery ticket too.

She held her breath for a second then laughed to herself when that didn't appear out of thin air.

Rosalinda was smiling from ear to ear when she left the little girl's room. And something else amazing began to happen. The worry she'd been feeling since Joaquin was admitted felt just a bit smaller. She shut the door gently behind her and went on to the next room.

After she finished delivering all the gifts to the children's rooms, she wheeled the cart to the nurses' station. There were several on duty and they looked exhausted. Most had come on duty at 7:00pm, but with the holiday, others were covering shifts for those that had the holiday off. With a sneaky smile, Rosalinda picked up the small presents and put one in front of each nurse.

Somehow, she knew the names of each one, without looking at their badges, and which present went to who.

"What's this?" Nurse Jane asked, looking around. "Who put this here? I didn't even see anyone come up to me." Everyone else shook their heads and then looked down in wonder to see their own gifts, their names neatly printed on each tag. Rosalinda almost wanted to watch them open the gifts, but a quick look at the clock reminded her she still had two more floors to go. She got back on the elevator and hit the button 4.

It felt like she'd been walking for hours but every time she looked at a clock, she was surprised at how little time had actually passed. Besides the numbered presents, she also delivered the ones she brought from home. The closer it got to midnight, the more she wanted to see the looks on the children's faces when they realized that Santa had been to visit. She would have to settle for Joaquin's face, but she would be more than happy for that.

It was one minute before midnight when she delivered the last present, saving the final delivery for Joaquin's room. She picked up the final gift box and the cart wavered in the air, shimmered, then dissolved before her eyes. She walked in his room and her heart sang at the sight of her husband, sleeping peacefully for the first time in over a week. She quietly set the present on his table and walked tired, but satisfied, to the padded bench under the window. She slipped off her shoes and slid them to the side. She positioned the pillow at one end and sat on the cushion. She stretched her arm and legs then laid down, pulling a sheet over herself.

She dreamed of Santa Claus.

"Merry Christmas!"

Rosalinda woke with a start. Joaquin was sitting up in bed as one of the food attendants, not the one from last night, set a tray on the rolling table and adjusted the height for Joaquin to eat. He lifted the dome from the plate to reveal scrambled eggs and bacon. A biscuit and glass of orange juice sat beside it on the tray.

"Did you need me to take that empty one away?" The attendant asked, pointing to the tray on the desk near Rosalinda.

"That's not mine." Joaquin replied, unwrapping the napkin containing his silverware. "Besides it says 'Rosalinda' on it."

"What?" Rosalinda looked over and saw a tray with a single domed plate and an identical box to Joaquin's.

She sat up and rubbed her eyes.

"What time did you get here?" Joaquin asked, taking a bite.

"It was really late, and you were asleep," she replied. "I didn't want to wake you."

"Did you sleep okay?" he asked her as he picked up the biscuit and began to butter it.

"I sure did," Rosalinda answered with a sly smile. "In fact, I fell asleep as soon as I got here."

"I wonder what's on your tray," Joaquin said curiously.

"Why don't you open yours first?" Rosalinda asked, setting the gifts closer to him.

As soon as he finished eating, he opened them all. He loved the books she bought him, he was an avid reader, and was happy to see another book by C. J. Peterson. He smelled the bottle of bacon scented hand lotion and immediately rubbed some into his dry hands.

"Now I smell like breakfast," he joked, then picked up the mysterious box that Santa had given to Rosalinda.

She leaned closer, curious as to what was inside the wrapping.

"This is gorgeous!" he exclaimed, holding up an angel wing pendan. "Now let's see what's in yours."

"I guess I will find out." Rosalinda stood up and took two steps to the desk.

She picked up the present and opened it. It was a matching angel wing. They'd been talking about getting these for their next anniversary. Yet here they were now.

She reached out and lifted the dome from the plate. It was a tiny cup of milk and three cookies.

"What does that mean?" Joaquin asked. "Does someone think you are Santa Claus?"

Rosalinda laughed. "Yeah, something like that."

Alone At Christmas

By:

Teresa Trent

Author Teresa Trent

Teresa Trent writes the Swinging Sixties Mystery Series, the Pecan Bayou and the Piney Woods Mystery Series. She has been a contributing author to many anthologies over the years. She lives in Houston, Tx and writes the Books to the Ceiling blog/podcast at TeresaTrent.blog.

https://teresatrent.com

Alone at Christmas

❦

There was an enormous gaping hole the wind could whistle through my heart, and nobody cared. Without my twin around, it felt like that. Stephanie and I had lived together all our lives. When we lost first one and then the other parent, we worked hard to observe the same holiday traditions. The first Christmas without them, we put up the tree and cried with the placing of each ornament. I'll admit, I cried more than my sister did, but most of those ornaments meant something.

With twins, there's often a more assertive one, and that was my sister, Stephanie. She said my tears were silly. I was being maudlin. To me it was a way to heal and move on with my life. I was stronger for it. Now, the emptiness I felt when we lost our parents had once again returned, and I wasn't sure how I would get through it this time without her.

She didn't even look at me as they pulled out of the driveway. Her last explanation had been very matter of fact. "You see, Mara, we're in love. You know we've been in love since summer and, well, we've wanted to move in together. You can understand that, can't you? You know I love you, but it's time we both started living our lives separately." She ran her hand through her short brown hair. She kept telling me how practical short hair was, and after a while she talked me into it. We had always looked the same, been the same in every way. That was until Joey came on the scene.

Joey was a contractor who helped us spruce up our parent's house to sell. I should have noticed how close they were getting. For months Stephanie couldn't stop talking about him. It was out of the norm for my sister to be so daffy. She would describe herself as a hard-edged realist. I guess even with Stephanie, love makes fools of us all. But now, I was standing alone in the little house we rented once our parent's home sold. Our Christmas tree was half decorated and the quiet in the house made me feel lonely.

I tried to talk myself out of the darkness that was encroaching on my mood. She was gone, and I was welcome to do whatever I wanted to celebrate the holiday by myself. Whatever that would be. I closed the door and gave in to a rush of tears. How could I ever get through this? I put on one of our parents' CDs and picked up a red strand of glittery garland. Halfheartedly, I draped it across the tree in a way that my sister had always told me was the artistic approach to doing it. Even though Stephanie wasn't in the room, her observations were still haunting me. Would it be like this from now on? Would I constantly ask myself what would Stephanie do? After a few more ornaments were on the tree, my sister usually made hot chocolate. Somehow, I wasn't thirsty for it. Stephanie and Joey were putting up their tree tonight, and I wished so much I could be a part of their celebration.

I was pathetic, but the thought of not spending Christmas Eve alone inspired me. I could knock on their door and tell her she forgot something. I manically searched around the house looking for anything, anything at all that she might have forgotten, and finally came up with a scarf. It was a thick red wool and went well with our coloring. She liked to borrow it from me, and I could give it to her as a housewarming gift.

Five minutes later, I parked my car in the driveway of their tiny bungalow. The front curtains were open. The Christmas tree wasn't lit, so it stood like a black outline against the white walls behind it. Their home was in a busier section of town and was surrounded by a few bars and trendy restaurants. It was a gentrified neighborhood for the up-and-coming crowd.

I had exited the car, scarf in hand, when my sister stepped in front of the window holding a crystal ornament. The light in the room caught her face. She looked so happy, that a rush of guilt came over me for trying to force myself into this moment. Joey came up behind her and put his arms around her waist and nuzzled at her neck. There was no way I would break up this romantic evening. What had I been thinking? Deep in my heart, I secretly hoped she had acted too hastily and would come back to the home that we shared. From the look of desire in her eyes, I didn't see that happening tonight. I loved Stephanie, even though I felt betrayed by her moving out on me. I couldn't take this away from her. I turned back to my car to return to my half-decorated sad-sack tree.

There was a sniffling sound coming from the bushes.

My gaze landed on a small form crouched down and crying. It was a little boy with his hood pulled up. When he tried to adjust it, I noticed he only had one mitten. He couldn't have been more than seven and when he saw me, he backed up slightly.

"Are you OK?" I asked.

He answered with more tears. I approached him slowly, then bent down to get a better look at him. He didn't seem hurt, but he was shivering in the frosty night air. "Where's your mother?"

"At her house."

"Why isn't she here with you?"

"It was dad's weekend, but now that's over. My aunt said Mom was going to meet us at Barney's Billiards, but then she didn't. She said something about a new boyfriend, and she told me to wait there for my mom. That was a long time ago. I walked down the street trying to see her, but now I don't know where I was supposed to wait."

"Do you want me to call your dad?"

"I'm not supposed to. My mom says the judge granted her this time, not him. It would make her mad."

"I don't think she would be thrilled that you are here all by yourself in the cold." As if on cue, the little boy shivered again. "Tell me his number and I'll call him. Or better yet, let me try to call your mother."

He quickly reeled off both numbers and I tapped them into my phone, but each time I connected, my calls went to voicemail. What kind of parents didn't answer their phones? Even if my number was unknown to them, you'd think they'd answer because of their child having to go between them.

"Well, I guess we've done all we can do. I know you don't know me, but could we go to my house to wait? It's cold out here." I glanced over at my sister's house. I could bring him in there, but if I did, I would have to explain how I was in the neighborhood and the scarf excuse seemed thin right now.

"I'm not supposed to go with strangers."

"I know. But we need to get out of the weather. How about if we go to some place public like the mall?"

"Would it mean I have to get in a car?"

"I'm afraid so. How about one of the restaurants here or we could go back to Barney's?"

"I don't know." He began to cry again. This was too much for him.

I glanced back up at my sister's new house. I would just have to face the embarrassment and bring him inside. "Come on. This is where my sister lives. We don't have to get into the car, and she looks just like me, so she doesn't even qualify as a stranger."

When we knocked on the door, it was a few minutes before anyone answered. My sister's eyes grew bigger as I stood there with my new little friend. "Mara? What are you doing here?" Archie stood beside me holding my hand with his mittened side.

"Hi, um. I was going to drop off this scarf, house-warming gift," I quickly explained, "and I ran into this little fellow in the bushes. He fell between the cracks when his parents were switching off custody for the evening. I've tried to call them but I'm afraid it went straight to voicemail. I'm sorry for barging in like this, but you were the closest place. I hope you don't mind."

Stephanie's eyes warmed as she took in the little boy. "What's your name?"

He looked up at me and then over at Stephanie. "You look alike."

"We're twins," I said.

He looked at us again and then grinned. "Cool. My name is Archie."

Stephanie stepped away from the door. "Well then, Archie, you'd better come in because I was about to make some hot chocolate. Would you like some?"

"Yes, ma'am."

Joey leaned toward Archie. "We've been working awfully hard on our tree tonight. Would you like to see some of our ornaments?"

"Sure."

Stephanie grabbed me by the arm and dragged me into the kitchen. It was homey, even with the boxes piled up against the wall. "What are you doing? I knew you wouldn't be able to leave me alone on Christmas Eve, but I never expected you to kidnap an orphan."

"He's not an orphan. I found him wandering around outside your house. He was left in front of Barney's Billiards and nobody came to pick him up."

"Then you ought to call children's services." She grabbed a pan out of a box and poured milk from a carton she retrieved from the refrigerator into it. She added a liberal dose of cocoa and some sugar from another box.

"Don't you think that's a little drastic? I'm sure one of his parents will call me back eventually."

"But they don't know who you are. With all the spam calls we all get, there's no way they're going to call you back. If he won't let you drive him to his house, did you leave your address on the voice mails? Have you done that?"

Out of the two of us, she was always the sensible one. The one who thought ahead.

"No," I mumbled.

"Man, of all the people for him to have had to be rescued by it had to be you."

"What is that supposed to mean?"

"Nothing."

She turned the burner on under the pan. "I think you should call the police. They could be here to pick him up in the next hour."

"And if I do that, I'll get his parents in trouble."

"And the problem with that is? You need to do your civic duty and get this boy into proper supervision. It's obvious the parents don't care for him if they lose track of him on Christmas Eve."

"Do I dial the police station or 911?"

"911. This is an emergency. They left a child alone in the cold."

She spoke like any idiot would know this and I didn't appreciate it. When the dispatcher answered, I described our situation and she let out a sigh."

"I'd really like to help you, but it is Christmas Eve if you haven't noticed. I'll put the message out, but I can't guarantee when anybody will be there to pick him up. People like to go out and party on Christmas Eve or get into fights with their relatives. All that holiday spirit is keeping our officers busy."

I thanked her and hung up. "Are you happy now?"

"Yes. I'm amazed you're concerned about my happiness. You show up here with the excuse that you came by to drop off a scarf. Like anyone believes that."

She was right. It was a poor excuse to come visit her, but if the little boy hadn't shown up, I would have turned around and gone home. She never would have known.

"You know what your problem is? You're lonely. You've never learned how to live life outside of being a twin. You had to know that this would happen eventually. I'm in love with Joey, and I intend to live with him without you."

She was right. She deserved her happiness. "Fine. Don't worry about me. I'm going to go check on Archie, but first I'm going to call both parents again and leave your address. That's OK, isn't it?"

She was back to stirring the pan, then raised the other hand dismissively. "Whatever."

I made the calls and then walked in, seeing Joey raising Archie to the top to put the star on the tree. In the background, I heard The Chipmunks singing about Christmas as the tree twinkled in the now darkened room. The moment was magical and what this little guy should have had spending Christmas Eve with his parents.

"Beautiful. You guys did a wonderful job!" I had misjudged Joey. He would make a great dad someday.

Joey put Archie down.

"It's awesome!" Archie said, raising his hands in the air. He was quite the contrast to the little boy shivering in the bushes. He walked over and hugged me around the waist, then let go. "Thank you for letting me come to your Christmas."

"Well, it's not really my Christmas," I glanced at Stephanie, bringing a tray of mugs into the room. "It's my sister's, but I'm really glad you're here too. I'm just sorry you're not doing this with your mom. I'll bet she has a beautiful tree."

Archie took a mug and sipped. When he smiled back, he had a whipped cream mustache. "She doesn't have a tree. She works a lot."

"Oh, I'm sorry."

"My dad has one, though. We put it up two weeks ago. Just us men." Archie nodded, proud of that.

"So right," Joey said, putting out a large hand to high five. Balancing the mug, Archie gently placed his little hand on Joey's palm.

"I wished I could be here instead of with my mom. She likes to take naps when I'm there." In the background the Chipmunks had launched into their version of "All I Want for Christmas is My Two Front Teeth".

"I'll bet your mom is worried about you right now." Stephanie put her hand on Archie's shoulder. "Don't you worry, though. We've called the police, so they'll come get you soon."

Archie's eyes widened. "The police? Am I being arrested? What'd I do?"

My sister loved to make sure everyone had an uncomfortable grip on reality.

I shot Stephanie a look. "No, Archie. You didn't do anything wrong. Stephanie just thought they might have better luck getting you to your parents."

He took another drink of the hot chocolate as if he didn't want to leave a drop if he were to be carted away in a patrol car. "I don't want to go with the police."

I did my best to reassure him. "I'm sure one of your parents will get here first."

He turned and motioned for me to get down on his level, face to face. "I'll go in your car now. I want to live with you when I'm not with my dad."

I had been feeling so lonely and unwanted, but this little boy was willing to turn his whole life upside down for me. "That is so sweet, but I don't think your mother, or the judge, would approve, do you? Let's just be happy we're here drinking hot chocolate and looking at this beautiful tree."

"I wouldn't be any trouble," he offered. "I promise. Do you have other kids?"

"Sorry, champ, I don't."

There was a pounding at the door, that, had I been holding my hot chocolate, I would have made a mess all over Stephanie's carpet.

"You think that's the police?" I asked. "I thought they only pounded on the door like that when they were about to raid the place."

"I'll get it," Joey said, puffing out his chest slightly.

When he opened the door, a tall man bundled up in a gray wool scarf, and wearing a black parka, moved past him. "Archie?"

"Daddy!" He ran to his father's arms and upon embrace was picked up, his feet dangling in midair.

"How did you get here? Where's your mother?"

"I don't know. She never came for me." He turned back to us. "Look at our tree! I put the star on top."

The man set his son down and pulled down his scarf. "Looks great."

I stepped forward. "I found him out in the bushes by himself. I was, uh, visiting my sister and he was freezing out there, so I brought him inside with me. I hope that's okay."

His gaze met mine. His eyes matched his scarf, a charcoal grey. His hair was a deep brown, cut short. "Thank you so much for taking him in." He turned back to Archie. "What did I tell you about strangers?"

"I know, and I didn't get in her car."

He shook his head and tweaked his son on the nose. "You're lucky this lady saw you and wasn't one of the bad ones."

"She's beautiful," Archie leaned closer in a mock whisper. "And there's two of her."

His father looked at me again with those eyes and then found Stephanie standing next to Joey. "I'll be darned. There are." He took off his glove and extended his hand in my direction. "I'm Jon Martin and I can't thank you enough."

As his skin touched mine, I felt something. It couldn't be an instant attraction. That just didn't happen, but something. "I'm Mara and this is my sister Stephanie and her boyfriend Joey."

"Thanks for letting him spend Christmas at your house."

"Oh, it's not my house. Stephanie lives here. I was just stopping by to bring her a scarf."

The corners of his mouth turned up a bit. "Really? On Christmas Eve?"

Stephanie scowled. "That's what I said. Can I get you some hot chocolate? We called the police too, so they ought to be here any minute."

"I see. I guess we'd better wait."

"Or I could just call them back and cancel it," I suggested. Stephanie seemed a little startled I came up with the solution before she could.

"I like that better," Jon said.

I quickly called 911 and canceled the call telling them the boy's father had picked him up. All a big misunderstanding. The operator seemed relieved. "Yeah, yeah. Merry Christmas."

"All fixed."

Archie let out a breath. "Does this mean they aren't going to arrest me and take me to the orphan's home?"

Jon zipped up Archie's coat. "If they arrest anyone, it will be your mother and her sister. I knew there was a new man in her life. She probably thinks her sister kept you. She does that sometimes."

"Maybe you should call her, so she doesn't come to my home demanding her child?" Stephanie inserted.

"Of course. Thanks again." Jon looked down at Archie. "Say goodnight, son. I guess we get to spend Christmas together after all."

"Mom won't be happy."

"Well, she should have thought of that before she trusted your care to her sister." He turned to me. "I, uh, think you made quite an impression on my son."

"She did," Archie interrupted. "I want to stay with her when I'm not with you, okay Dad?"

"Uh, we'll have to talk about that," he expertly avoided committing to his son's plan like any diplomatic dad would. "I have to say, if my son had to be rescued, he couldn't have picked a prettier heroine."

With that, he turned and left my sister's house.

As Stephanie closed the door, she scowled. "Weirdo. A *prettier heroine*. What is this? Bridgerton? Guys like that, a dime a dozen. What kind of loser marries a woman who forgets to pick up her kid on Christmas Eve?"

I listened to Stephanie continue to trash Jon and for the first time, her view of the situation didn't seem right. I had been thrilled, even happy with his words, but she said he was a weirdo. He didn't seem like a loser. He seemed like a man in a tricky situation. It was almost as if she enjoyed being the one who got all the good things. I grabbed my coat. "Thanks for the hot chocolate. Got to go."

I looked out on the street where a white SUV was parked on the street. Jon was still strapping Archie into his car seat. I made my way down the sidewalk, now getting icy as snow fell around us.

"Right." Stephanie shouted from the door as she put her arm through Joey's. "And thanks for crashing our first holiday together."

"No problem." I walked directly to Jon's car, where he was putting his gloves on.

Stephanie's voice cut through the air. "What are you doing? That's not your car."

"I'm doing what you told me to do. I'm living my life without you."

"Don't be crazy," she called after me. "You should go home. It's late. This is way too much excitement for you."

"Well, hi." Jon said, turning around with a pleasant smile.

"I'm Mara."

"You told me that."

"I know you just met me, but would you like to get dinner sometime?"

Archie piped up. "I would!"

Jon laughed. "Well, then. I guess I would, too. We're a matched pair, you know. Family has to stick together."

"That's what I've always thought, too."

We hope you enjoyed
these heart-warming
stories by some
amazing authors!
May this Christmas
season bring you and
yours many blessings!

Merry Christmas
and Happy New Year!

Texas Sisters Press, LLC
https://texassisterspress.com
"Quality books for the family."